RECKONING

THE WATCHERS

BOOK SIX

VERONICA WOLFF

ALSO AVAILABLE

IN THE WATCHERS SERIES

Isle of Night

Vampire's Kiss

Blood Fever

The Keep

Dark Craving

Reckoning

RECKONING

IN THE GAME OF EVIL, THERE IS ALWAYS A
FINAL RECKONING

Annelise's slaying of Vampire Dagursson has thrown the Isle of Night - and her own heart - into chaos. Though she shares a bond with the vampire Carden, her connection to Ronan grows deeper as he protects her from those who seek justice for and power from Dagursson's death.

But there's one thing Ronan can't protect her from - his sister, Charlotte, who is alive and sworn to destroy Annelise and everyone she holds dear. Now Annelise must decide who she trusts as she embarks on a suicide mission to rescue the most important woman she's never met: her mother.

Trapped in a deadly game against an ancient evil, not everyone will be left standing as Annelise faces the final reckoning.

Dedicated to Barbara Freethy, friend through thick, thin, and extra thin.

CHAPTER ONE

"You have changed my life. Given me hope." His hand traced down my side, dipped to my waist. Stroked along my hip and down my thigh. "You are light where there was only darkness."

I turned into him. We lay on my bed in the shadows. His eyes, even in the dimness of moonlight, were haunted. It was dark, and yet I could call to mind their deep green color as easily as I could the shape of my own hand. He was mortal and only a couple of years older than me, but sometimes those eyes made him seem as ancient as any vampire.

That gaze was heavy on me now. Drawn to me only.

"Ronan," I whispered.

But he was done with talking. He pulled me closer and kissed me softly. I savored the feel of lips I could draw from memory. How long I'd studied every inch of that face, and yet so few days had passed since it'd been mine to touch.

He drew back. Those eyes, so soulful and all-seeing, remained locked on me. "Why are you with him when you should be with me?"

My throat clenched. *Carden.* My affection for the ancient

Scottish vampire ran deep. The bond I shared with him infused my blood.

But this thing I felt for Ronan, it went beyond chemical. It penetrated a secret heart I didn't realize I had.

Ronan must've seen the thoughts flicker across my face because he brushed the hair from my forehead, as though he might sweep my mind clear. "Let's run away. We'll disappear. Live in some faraway place." His voice was suddenly husky with intensity.

"But I'm…"

I was…what? In love with Carden?

Was I? How was that possible when all my mind could summon was Ronan?

"I'm with Carden," I said finally. We shared a bond—a bond that might endanger me were it severed.

He pulled away completely then and rolled onto his back, leaving a Ronan-sized chill along one side of my body.

"You're with Carden because you bonded," he told me, his voice tight. "By accident. It's naught more than a chemical reaction. You might as well be bonded to a drug. It's your blood that calls for Carden." He swung that tormented gaze back to me, and it was like the tide, mysterious and powerful, drawing me more deeply to him. "But your heart? Tell me, Ann. What does your heart tell you?"

"My heart?" My heart pumped blood that was bonded to Carden. To cut that bond would be to endure the blood fever. "There's no way around it," I said finally. Desperately. "The blood fever…"

I'd been parted once before from my vampire. The physical effects were devastating.

Ronan's hand flew to my face, cupping my cheek. "The blood fever I can soothe."

The hope in his voice cracked something inside me.

"How?" Even as I said it, I knew. I took his hand in mine. "Your touch."

Ronan had the power of persuasive touch. It was what he used to convince kids like me to come to this island of death. The vampires identified us—teenaged misfits, runaways, addicts, those of us who wouldn't be missed—but it was Tracers like Ronan who traveled the world, hunting us, bringing us to the Isle of Night. Different Tracers had different strengths, and Ronan's was his touch—when he used it, it was enough to persuade anyone to do anything.

I rolled away. "Your touch could help, sure, but for how long? You'd soothe the blood fever, but eventually—"

"It could be gone forever. If you let me try." He took my arm and pulled me back into the shelter of his body. "I'm strong, Ann. Stronger than you know."

He was strong. Could he be that strong?

Before, I wouldn't have thought so. But recently I'd seen him unleash his power on a vampire. It'd almost been enough to overcome one as ancient as Master Dagursson. Might it be enough to completely sever a blood bond?

"You must let me try, at least. Think, Ann. You could be parted from him forever. Let me do this for you." His tone grew earnest then. "For once, let me use my power for good."

I'd never heard him sound so vulnerable. I'd always known Ronan despised the work he was forced to do. Increasingly, he let me in enough to see just how deeply his hatred ran.

"But how..." The words came so slowly, my mouth frozen. "How..."

I couldn't get the words out. Why was my jaw so leaden? My tongue so thick?

"Be easy," I heard. There were hands on me. Cool hands. "Be easy, lass."

I opened my eyes. I was in Carden's arms.

My pulse gave a sharp, defensive kick.

"What...?" I glanced around, trying to make sense of this.

And then my heart plummeted. Just a dream.

"Hush, dove. You were dreaming." Carden snuggled me closer and placed his palm over my heart. "Your blood races." His hand swept from my chest and down along my belly, coming to rest heavy over the very core of me. "Was it me you dreamt of?"

My cheeks burned, and I was grateful for the darkness. Slowly my heartbeat returned to normal. Still, it felt as though it was pumping air, not blood.

Guilty guilty guilty. Ronan had shocked me when he'd stolen two kisses, and apparently they were still at the forefront of my mind. The forefront of my *everything*.

He'd kissed me, and I'd kissed him back, and I could never, ever tell. I dared not even think about it. If Carden were to find out, he very well might kill him.

"You expect me to say? A girl has to maintain some mystery." I gave him a saucy smile but had to force my lips not to tremble.

His hand skimmed down and around, curling beneath my thigh, and then he swooped me atop him. "Indeed?" He returned my smile. It was wicked and roguish.

Was I imagining the distance in his eyes? Carden was of an ancient Celtic line from which he'd inherited tremendous intuitive powers. Had he sensed he wasn't the one who haunted my dreams?

I panicked as I bent down to kiss him.

Honestly, it was no great hardship.

Handsome Carden. He was as noble as any knight. Fierce as any warrior. He'd been only nineteen when he turned Vampire hundreds of years ago. His youthful body was frozen in time, and yet his heart was ancient, righteous, belonging to a hero of old.

And that heart loved me. It was intoxicating.

He kissed me back, eagerly, gruffly. There was a growl in his throat. "That's more like it, my beautiful wee firebrand."

Unable to stop an abrupt laugh, I sat up, straddling him. He'd called me "dove," "petal," "sunshine," "bonny," and once, "hen." But never "firebrand."

"Am I that much of a troublemaker?" I asked, but a fresh pang of guilt made me queasy. *If only he knew.*

"Oh, aye. In the most magnificent of ways." He threaded his fingers through my hair and pulled me back to him. The humor in his eyes was smoldering into something hotter. "And now it's time for show, not tell."

He kissed me again, but as he did, a part of my mind spun out of my control. Why had I let Ronan kiss me when I had *this*? Carden was wonderful. So why, in my dreams, did Ronan kiss me still?

Carden's mouth moved along my jaw and then whispered in my ear. "Where have you gone, sweetest one?"

He was immortal. Powerful. Impossibly so. He placed me above all others. Who wouldn't want to be with such a creature?

And yet Ronan kept a hold on me.

Which one was true? Which one was love?

For the dozenth time, I shoved such thoughts from my mind. Dreams were just that—fantasies based in unreality. Even if it was the wishful thinking of my unconscious mind, it wasn't real. And those kisses Ronan and I had shared now felt like no more than that—dreams. He hadn't even stayed afterward. He'd said he was going away, and I didn't even know to where.

But Carden was here, beneath me.

"I'm right here," I told him as I speared my fingers through his hair to pull his mouth close for another kiss.

I needed to be with Carden. This was crazy.

With Ronan, it'd been just a couple stolen moments. Carden and I had shared so much more. I adored him. He'd told me he loved me, and I believed him.

And like that I was lost to my thoughts again. Before I realized what was happening, Carden had stopped kissing me. We were laying side by side. Yet another moment lost to my overthinking. "Wait." I propped up on my elbow. "Where are you going?"

Now he was getting up. Donning his plaid.

From faraway came the distant gong of the dawn bell.

"I must hurry," he said. "And you must lie low. That pup Ronan has set the whole isle to chaos. Killing Dagursson as he did...he made a mess of it." He *tsked*.

But ultimately that'd been my mess. *I* was the one who'd killed Dagursson. In letting people believe he was the culprit, Ronan was protecting *me*.

I'd stolen the misericordia from Sonja, the ruler of *Eyja næturinnar*, this Isle of Night. It was the rarest of weapons, a dagger that could both make and kill vampires, and I'd used it to destroy one of the most powerful vampires on this island. It was only a matter of time before Sonja realized it was gone.

At great risk to his own life, Ronan had taken the blade off my hands. He'd told me how any vampire—Carden included—would do anything to have it for their own ends. He had insisted I not tell anyone about it or the part I'd played in Dagursson's death. Seeing as Ronan had risked all to direct attention away from me, I had to honor his wishes. I'd keep our secret.

All our secrets.

Yet another secret I kept from my vampire. Yet more guilt.

Carden sat on the bed to lace up his boots. "With Dagursson dead, there is a power vacuum."

It took me a second to follow the topic change.

"And you know how nature loves a vacuum," I joked weakly. It was all I could muster. This chat with Carden was skirting every single white lie I'd ever told. It was pretty unsettling.

Dagursson had allied with Ronan's sister, Charlotte. Charlotte, who was probably out there this minute, plotting my untimely death. She was a vampire now, and Ronan had been as shocked as I was when she'd appeared. Apparently, she was a little sassier—and a lot deadlier—than when he'd last seen her.

I tried to calm myself. "But Dag was just a weirdo etiquette teacher, right? So he'd been in charge of the scrolls—he can't have been the only vampire who's able to translate those things. How does his death change anything?"

Carden pinned me with an uncharacteristically grave look. "Don't mistake me. I dance on that Viking bastard's grave, but his death brings instability. There are those who've chosen sides, who are making their secret loyalties known."

"Secret loyalties?" Why was my face burning? Sure, I had a secret or two, but it wasn't a "secret loyalty."

"Aye, not all support Fournier," he said, referring to the headmaster of the Isle. "Perhaps not even Alcántara. And it seems some of those scrolls are missing. The pup thinks to steal the lore for himself."

This was news to me. I knew Ronan had burned a couple of Dagursson's scrolls, precious for the knowledge they held about genealogies and vampire blood lines. But had he returned to the scene of the crime to pilfer more?

"I never thought Ronan the power-hungry sort," Carden said with a shake of his head. "So what is he thinking?" He pinned a sudden look on me. "Is that pup doing an errand for you?"

"Stop calling him 'pup.'" My voice was sharper than I'd intended. I forced my next words to come out calm and even. "What kind of errand would he do for me, anyway?"

"Your mother," he said, going in a direction I hadn't expected. "Those scrolls might lead him to her."

"Could they?" I felt a familiar spike in my chest—the waning and waxing of hope and despair. "What would the scrolls have to do with my mother? They're old as dirt, and she can't be much older than forty."

"Aye, but word is, she's kept company with those who are even more ancient than I."

Carden had recognized my mother from a photo. For weeks, I'd thought he'd disappeared, but he'd actually gone in search of her. He'd found only a cold trail, but for me it was enough. Now that I knew she might be alive, my dream, above all else, was to find her.

"We could look for her," I said. "You and me." I stared at him in the dawning light. He was steadfast and affectionate. Caring and carefree. He was incredibly appealing, and I adored him. He'd been there for many of my darkest hours with that rakish smile and easy laugh. "We could run away. We'd be together. We could be happy."

The words left the taste of dust in my mouth, so much an echo of what Ronan had said to me in the dream. But I couldn't imagine either of them wanting to run away, much less with me.

I swung my legs over the side of the bed, wanting to challenge him. To actually *see* that he loved me rather than merely hear the words. "We'll leave here. Find my mother. Then run off somewhere and just...be."

His gaze became distant at the mention of my mother. All

thoughts of love fled as I suddenly feared that he was hiding something about her.

"What?" Maybe my mother didn't want to see me, didn't want to be found. I hadn't seen her since I was four. Years change a person. And why had she left in the first place? "What does that look mean? Do you know something?"

"Only that it's too soon." He scooted closer to me and spoke gently. "Things need to settle here before we make any moves. The Directorate is on alert. We couldn't leave now."

"But...if things are so unsettled, isn't it a good time to leave?" I mustered a smile, wondering what he wasn't saying.

His eyes were shuttered. "There's much to do yet. Much that keeps me here." But then, as if a light switched on inside him, his attention for me returned. "Our day will come."

Our day will come. Why did I hear something else in those words? Something that went beyond our relationship to encompass the balance of power on *Eyja næturinnar*.

CHAPTER TWO

The Isle's rigorous academic schedule stopped for nothing, not even the murder of one of its most celebrated instructors. It was the Advanced Combatives seminar for me that morning. But not even a few good knocks upside the head could jar the dark thoughts from me, and I left class feeling defeated. Not that I was beaten by any challenger. I'd become pretty accomplished at sparring and was well on my way to ascending to Guidon. No, it was my emotional demons that had me fighting for my life.

First, there was Ronan. Would we ever talk about what had happened between us? He'd taken off to who-knew-where and was probably in all kinds of danger because of what I did. Meanwhile, his sister, Charlotte, was out there somewhere. Only now she was a vampire, and she was gunning for me.

And then there was Yasuo. My oldest friend on the island was becoming Draug—a brand of mindless demon that had the reasoning power of a goat and the temperament of a rabid jackal. And yeah, once again, *my* fault. It was my fault he was becoming that way, his mind broken after watching his girlfriend, Emma, sacrifice herself for me in one of Alcántara's sick competitions.

Emma. My best friend who might or might not be out there even now, somewhere, suffering.

Then there was my mother. Apparently she *was* alive out there, but my boyfriend, my maybe-bonded-for-all-time vampire, wouldn't take me to find her yet.

And what about Carden? Would I feel this strongly about him without the blood bond we shared? Was our connection permanent, or had my dreaming mind been onto something? Could Ronan really soothe my blood fever and help me break the bond?

Was that even what I wanted?

I couldn't deal with any of that right now, but there was one thing I could do: check in on Yasuo. His transition from cute, floppy-haired LA boy into Draug was almost complete. Recently, he'd stopped coming onto campus altogether. But I knew where to find him.

My destination was a steep ridge that rose like a gnarled spine from the center of the Isle. I didn't know what about that place called to him, but I often found him there, just sitting and staring.

I skipped lunch and made my way through the most barren part of the island. The dimming was imminent, that time of the year when the sun skimmed the horizon and would not fully rise again for weeks. Soon the sky would be a relentless slate gray, neither dark nor light. It made my skin itch with longing...for darkness, for daylight...for something.

As I clambered up the last rocky bit, sure enough, there was Yasuo. It was weird, though. He was sitting in the middle of the trail, like he'd just stopped and dropped. He could've sat on top of one of the boulders surrounding us. A slight shift to the northeast and he would have had a lovely view of Crispin's

Cove in the distance. But no, he was just stopped in the middle of the gravel. Gray below, gray above.

It didn't matter to me, though. I was just happy to have a chance to see him. Every once in a while, I'd catch a glimmer of the old Yas. The way he'd sometimes rake his hand through his hair. How his long legs twined like a pretzel when he sat, making him seem like a giant kid. It threw me back to a time when he was human, and we were friends. Best friends.

Him, Emma, me.

I gave a little cough, as much to clear the emotion from my throat as to warn him of my approach. "Hey, Yas," I said, sitting down beside him.

He didn't speak to me. That was happening more and more. Disturbingly, this time he didn't even seem to be looking at anything. His dead eyes just aimed straight ahead.

It was awkward, sitting in the middle of the trail on a slight incline, but I angled myself even more toward him, trying to catch his eye. Awareness prickled up my spine, putting my back to the open like that, but I was desperate to connect.

"Look, Yas. I brought you something from breakfast." I fished a slice of bread wrapped in a napkin from my coat pocket. It was a rare treat, one he'd always loved. "Bread with currants. Your favorite, right?" I held it out to him.

His gaze didn't waver. He didn't even budge.

Whether or not he had thoughts in that head, I'd never know. I'd stopped trying to communicate in any meaningful way with him weeks ago. I was just happy that he'd stopped trying to kill me.

I placed the bread in his lap. With a twinge, I realized that he wasn't wearing a coat, despite the biting chill in the air. One more notch of his humanity gone.

But I'd fight it. Ronan had the misericordia, and if that blade could make vampires, maybe it could unmake Draug.

I patted his leg. "I have to assume you're in there somewhere, Yas. I need you to be in there. There must be some cure for you, and until—"

"Hey, little girl." A voice, faint and teasing on the wind, startled me. "Can I join your party?"

"Crap," I whispered. I'd *known* it was stupid to expose my back. I looked around, extending my senses, trying to determine if this voice belonged to friend or foe.

"Language, young Acari." The voice was closer now. It belonged to a woman. "The rocks have ears."

Where was it coming from? I rose to my knees. My hands were poised over my stars, but I tried to keep my tone light. "How is it I always feel so alone, yet I seem to be constantly surrounded by—"

And then I saw her. Charlotte.

Not friend. Enemy.

Ronan's sister stood high atop the ridge behind us, dark hair and dark cloak flapping in the wind. She was every inch the avenging beauty.

Last I saw her, she'd been raging at me. I'd killed Dagursson, and who'd have guessed anyone would've chosen to ally with such a megacreeper as that ancient Viking?

Carden's words reverberated in my memory: *There are those who've chosen sides, who are making their secret loyalties known.*

I'd killed Dag, and Charlotte wanted me to suffer for it. The only reason I was still alive was because Ronan had been with me. He'd stopped his sister from hurting me.

But now I was alone. Correction—I spared a quick glance at Yasuo—just as good as alone. Was I strong enough to take her down?

"Do finish, Annelise. Or do I call you Drew? That's what people close to you call you, isn't it? And I have a feeling we're going to get *very* close before this is done." She gave me an evil little smile, fangs gleaming despite the gray half-light. "You said you're constantly surrounded by...?"

I attempted a weak smile. "By things that want me dead."

This was Ronan's sister. His *sister*. The one he'd adored, the only link to his past.

Cold plumes of dread wended through me. If she attacked me, could I really kill her?

I couldn't. I wouldn't. She was quite possibly Ronan's last surviving family member. He was too important to me to go there.

But her cold gaze told me that I wasn't going to be winning her over with my humor any time soon.

She narrowed her eyes. "I'm a 'thing,' am I?" She stood on that rock, hands on hips, all towering malice. "But you were right about something: I do want you dead, little girl."

Maybe I could disable her somehow. Or at least try to talk her out of this standoff. Charlotte was a tall sip of badass. I was often stupid—something her brother liked to remind me of daily—but not stupid enough to fight her. Any fight with her would be my last, especially now that I no longer had the misericordia.

I stood and brushed off my hands. "I'm sure if you just wait ten minutes, some other creature will show up and do the dirty work for you."

She gave me an exaggerated pout. "But dirty work is so fun."

I forced a relaxed laugh. Just two gals sharing a joke. I did it to buy time, because I saw the shimmer of her urumi around her waist and knew she was stronger than I was. Far stronger.

I decided to try to appeal to the Charlotte she'd been when she was younger. Deep down, Ronan loved that part of her. "Look, we both care about Ronan. Surely we can find some common ground."

"Common ground?" She leapt from the boulder, dropping directly in front of us.

She had a violent glint in her eye, and I wriggled my wrists ever so slightly, feeling for the homemade stakes tucked there. Ironically, it'd been her brother who'd given me the idea to make them. Did I think I could manage to stake her? Ronan's sister or not, I was beginning to think I might enjoy the effort.

She trilled a merry, chiming laugh, which hardened into a sneer as her eyes landed on my forearms. "Look at you. You think you could kill me with your crude toys? Who do you think gave Ronan the idea in the first place?"

I shrugged, letting a stake slide low enough to rest in my palm. "I like the feel of them, all the same."

She gave me an appraising look. "I see you have a backbone. Perhaps I'll tear it out through your mouth."

"Now that's just gross."

She smiled. "Don't worry. I'll do it slowly so you're aware of every second."

It was official: she was totally insane. If I was going to face her, I needed a clear head, which meant I had to get Yasuo out of there.

I stepped in front of him and nudged him with my heel. "Get up, Yas. Time for you to go."

"Yo, D. What you kicking me for?" It was Yasuo. The *old* Yasuo. He always used to call me by some nickname or other, like "Blondie" or "D," short for "Drew," my last name. His voice was small, but it hit me with the force of a blow.

Charlotte's eyes lit up and shot to Yasuo behind me. "Well, well. Look who decided to join us."

I edged away from him. I needed Charlotte's attention on me. "Yasuo has nothing to do with this. This is between you and me."

Her eyes flew back to meet mine. "It's about so much more

than you and me, little girl. More fool you for believing otherwise." Slowly, she raised her arm to reach up and behind her. Was she hiding a weapon? I took a fighting stance, and she laughed outright. "At ease, Acari. If I wanted you dead, you'd be dead."

I relaxed a little, but kept my arms slightly out, feeling a little like an Old West gunslinger. "What are you doing, then?"

"Oh, relax already. I have a little something for you." Her tone turned snarky. "A wee gift. Since we both care for my brother, aye?"

It was time to face this head-on. Something told me I needed to show some bravado if I wanted to stay alive—to look her in the eye or puff my feathers or whatever it was creatures did in the wild to warn their enemies they were not to be underestimated.

Killing Master Dagursson had felt empowering. I'd killed a powerful member of the Vampire Directorate, and yet here I was, still standing. I wasn't going to cower before these monsters anymore.

"Look," I said, my eyes tracking her every movement, "I get that you're pissed I killed Dagursson."

Her arm froze in midair. "You killed more than just Dagursson." She tilted her head and peered more closely at me. "At first I'd thought to kill you in return, but then I decided to have a bit of fun instead. You see, there are other ways to destroy someone like you."

I didn't like the sound of that.

I feigned boredom, all the while registering every flick of her gaze, every twitch of her fingers. "You're a vampire now. What's more fun for you than killing? We gonna have a slumber party?"

I needed to lead her away from Yasuo. His eyes had lost their focus again, leaving him completely tuned out and basically helpless. My gaze skittered around us, assessing my options. I couldn't turn and flee—I'd topple right over the sheer drop that was several yards behind me. There was a path behind the boulders, but Charlotte had those at her back. My only other escape route was the way I came from, which was too far away for me to make in a quick dash.

I was cornered.

It'd have to be a fight then. I flexed my calf, reaching for the reassuring pressure of my throwing stars. I needed a stronger base and shifted my feet slightly.

But first, I'd wait. I'd let her make the first move. I wouldn't go for it until she unsheathed her weapon. Her hands would be full, and I'd be able to sling my stars, one-two, right into her throat. It wouldn't kill her, but it sure would distract her, hopefully enough for me to make a break for it.

She'd give me a good chase, but it'd put space between me and Yasuo. And not to be a narcissist, but something told me I was the one who interested her.

My fingers tapped the air with the need to act. "Look, whatever you're up to, just get on with it. Or don't. Because I'd like to get back for dinner."

"Patience, brat." She fumbled behind her back. There was the tear of Velcro, followed by a look of peace and satisfaction on her face. "Here you go."

She raised her hand in triumph, and I startled. I'd been braced for a sword. But it wasn't a sword. It wasn't any sort of weapon at all.

My feet caught beneath me when it clicked.

She was holding a head.

A long tangle of hair hung from her clenched fist. The strands looked muddy in the shadowy half-light. No, not mud. Blood.

"I heard you were looking for your friend. Emma, was it?" She hoisted it higher. "Well, here she is."

The head swung. Slowly, it spun to a stop. Facing me.

And then I saw it. Saw *her*. Emma. There she was, mouth agape. Sightless eyes.

Screams filled my head...my screams. The burn of bile and tears seized my throat. Convulsively, I tried to gulp it all back.

I didn't realize I'd grabbed my throwing stars until I felt them cutting into my palms. I wanted to throw them, but didn't trust my trembling hands. "You...you're sick." The vampires were monsters, but there was something about this gesture that was more savage, more gruesome than anything they'd conjure. "What have you done?"

"Tit for tat, Drew. You presented me with Dagursson's body. And so I brought you a little something, too." She tossed Emma's head at me, and I jumped to miss it.

But Emma wasn't an *it*.

Oh God, Em. Sorry. I'm so sorry.

Should I gather the head, pay some respect? Only I couldn't bear to touch it, and that felt like the worst of betrayals.

Yasuo began to moan, and I spared him a quick glance. No, no he would *not* choose this moment to tune back into reality. "Don't look," I snapped.

"What? Didn't you want to see your friend? Though, I suppose in all fairness, it is just her head." Charlotte kicked at it, and an involuntary keening escaped my throat. "Not worth much without a body. But I can't account for everything." She gave a pleasant shrug. "You must agree, the urumi does a clean job on a neck. Would you like to see it in action?"

She leapt for me then. I threw two stars, and two more were in my hands in an instant. Her cloak made a *whup-whup* sound, and her urumi, the whiplike blade she carried, sang in the air, lashing out as she landed.

But she wasn't in front of me. I spun to face her...and met Charlotte's back.

With a single flick of her wrist, she'd slashed Yasuo's throat.

My eyes bugged from the surreal shock of it—it took half a second for it even to register. But then I was shouting, running to him. "Yas! Oh my God, Yas!"

Silently, my friend teetered. He dropped onto his side. Dead.

I shrieked and heaved his body toward me, but his clothes were already soaked with an apron of blood, a sickening mix of red with the sludge-black gore of the Draug. It was proof of how far gone Yasuo had been. He'd already become something less than human, and it broke my heart twice over. "What...why...what did you do?"

"What does it look like?" She was laughing. "Would you like to see me cut the head all the way off?"

"No...Jesus...what is wrong with you?" I hated the childlike pitch of my voice and the way it made me sound as broken as I felt. "Why are you doing this?"

"You cared about him." She was nonchalant as she whipped the urumi—once, twice—flicking Yas's blood from the blade. "And that was enough motivation for me."

"I'll kill you." I flew to my feet.

But Charlotte bristled, her weapon arm instantly poised and ready. "You move again and you die, little girl."

She was too close. She had me. I'd never be the one to land the first blow—which meant I'd never land any blow.

I looked from Charlotte back down to Yasuo. A single swish of that weapon was all it had taken to extinguish him. There wasn't even peace on his face. Just...blankness.

"Oh, Yas," I whispered. My tears were sudden, hot, and

very, very unwanted. I quickly scrubbed my face. "He wasn't a threat to you."

"Stop your simpering." She sauntered closer and nudged Yasuo's body with a booted toe. "These Draug are like walking sacks of rotted meat. A waste of resources, if you ask me. I did us all a favor."

The smell of his blood wafted up to me, thick and pungent. It bore the scent of something come from the sea to rot.

I locked my knees to steady my wobbly legs and made myself stand straight to face her. "Yas was just a kid. We all are. But you're some superpowerful vampire now. So why do you even care about us?"

Her brows shot up. "I told you. I care because you do, Drew." Her eyes narrowed, glinting with malice. "Just as I cared about Dagursson, my one link to finding my family. But you killed him, and his knowledge died with him. All hope of finding my family is gone."

"You have Ronan," I said with sudden intensity.

Because, *Ronan*. He should've been more than enough. Ronan was everything. How could she not see that?

Instead, she spat. Actually spat. "Ronan. Ridiculous. How is he my family when he chose you over me?"

"But...he didn't. He didn't choose me."

She peered at me. "Did he not?"

Words echoed in my memory. *"You're the girl my brother's in love with,"* Charlotte had said to me just before I'd killed Dag.

She sneered at my silence. "I wanted him to leave you. But when I told him you're his weakness, do you know what the fool said? He said you're his *strength*." She shook her head in disgust. "He stubbornly insists on protecting you. Siding with you. Choosing *you*."

Charlotte held up a hand to cut off my protests. "First you

took my brother, and when you killed Dagursson, you took the last chance I had at finding any others."

"So why don't you just kill me?" I angled my wrist and felt the satisfying shift of a stake easing into my left palm. "Then you'd have Ronan all to yourself."

"Oh, I will kill you." She smiled brightly. "But first, I'm going to destroy everyone you love. I'll take your people from you, one by one, as you've taken mine. And you're going to watch."

Adrenaline dumped into my veins. I did a mental scan of my few but treasured allies. Emma. Yasuo. A vice threatened to crush my chest, and I forced myself to breathe. I needed to focus. She clearly had something—and someone—in mind.

But who else would she kill for the sin of befriending me? Carden and Ronan were at the top of the list. I snarled, "Carden's too strong for you. And you wouldn't dare kill your only brother."

"You think? Whoever won't stand with me won't be left standing at all." She shrugged. "But Ronan will come around. Once he realizes what the stakes are, he'll decide I'm too important to him." She stepped closer. "But what really matters now is, who's important to *you*?"

"I've got no friends," I said, thinking dismally just how true that felt sometimes.

"Did I say friends? Emma, Yasss-whatever-his-name-was —they're only the beginning." Her eyes pierced mine. "Next stop, your mother."

My heart kicked into a gallop.

"What?" It came out as barely a whisper.

"You took everything from me. So now it's time for me to take from you."

A buzzing had begun in my head that my thoughts couldn't penetrate. "What do you know about my mother?"

"Turns out I know *a lot*." She grinned brightly. "She's being held prisoner— Oops!" Her eyes widened dramatically. "I slipped."

She knew my mother? It was impossible. "Prisoner? I don't believe you. Why would anyone imprison my mother?"

"Surely Carden told you." She stared at me in a moment of prolonged silence, then burst into tittering laughter. "You don't even know, do you? Oh, this will be a treat."

"You're lying." Carden had said he didn't know how to find her, and he wouldn't lie to me. It was Charlotte who lied. "I don't believe you."

"I can see that." She wiped her eyes, still shivering with amusement. "Tell you what: I'll let you know how to find her. I'll even give you a head start. But I'll get to her first. You'll be too late to help your dying mommy."

CHAPTER THREE

My mother. I had to save her. I had to leave. Now. No matter the cost.

But first, I had to find Carden.

I stormed to the dining hall. My vampire wasn't lying to me. It was impossible.

No, I'd find him and tell him what I'd learned. Charlotte told me my mother was being held prisoner by the Synod vampires in some faraway compound.

I knew those vamps. The Synod of Seven were a bunch of old-school German vampires, led by the baddest of them all, an ancient monk named Jacob, who made Alcántara look like The Count from *Sesame Street*. Jacob was the sort of guy who considered teetering stacks of skulls a decorating choice. Plus he had a penchant for ballroom dancing, and as far as I was concerned, it didn't get any more sadistic than that.

I'd saved Carden from Jacob's dungeon—it was how I'd first met my Scottish vampire. Carden had snapped Jacob's neck as we escaped, but Jacob was super old and super powerful, and something told me he wasn't dead.

Carden would want to go, I knew. And not just because it was me, and he'd want to help. He hated those vampires. He and I would leave, tonight. We'd save her together.

An intense surge of emotion wavered my vision as I thought of those I'd been unable to save. *Emma, Yasuo.* My best friends. I'd been unable to help them, though something deep inside me had known all this time that their fates had been sealed the day Emma chose not to fight me in Alcántara's brutal Directorate Challenge.

I just hadn't expected the final retribution to come from Charlotte. *Ronan's sister.* I still reeled from the discovery that she was alive. There'd been a day when Ronan had loved her— more than anything. He probably still did. Could I infiltrate Jacob's dungeons, rescue my mother, and maybe kill Ronan's only remaining family in the process?

I found Carden outside the dining hall, right where we'd agreed to meet. Back when my biggest concern had been things like memorizing verb declensions in old Norse and finishing my mythology paper on time.

A muscular arm snatched me from behind. "Such a face you pull, dove. Won't you give us a smile?"

I pulled away—I needed to get this out. "My mom is a prisoner?"

His face went blank.

My heart sank. "Wait, did you know that?"

"I know—"

My stomach churned. I'd thought Carden was always honest with me—but did that only apply to the things he chose to tell me? "You know? You *know*?"

"I know your mother is in no immediate danger." The cadence of his calm and measured words felt patronizing.

The clock was ticking. I didn't have time for patronizing. "Immediate danger—what does that even mean? No, Carden.

We need to leave, like, yesterday." He'd known this and hadn't told me? It made me feel lost. At a loss. I struggled to find my next words, but all that came out was, "What are you thinking?"

Even to my ears, my voice sounded shrill, and he snugged me close. "The walls have ears," he whispered. "Come, you must eat." He began to pull me into the dining room. "In any case, you can't go running off with an empty belly. I'll explain my mind over food."

Something hardened inside, and I pulled away. "Explain here."

A group of Trainees walked past, watching us intently.

Once again, Carden wrapped that hard arm around me. "You are surrounded by enemies. Now, come, sweet. We will act as we always do. You will nourish yourself, and we will discuss this calmly."

My traitorous belly fluttered with hunger. I hesitated, but the call of those shooters of blood I'd come to rely on was too strong, and I fell into step. "Fine. But we're going to make it quick. Then we're getting out of here."

I'd worried the dining hall wouldn't be the best setting to have a confidential conversation, but as we entered and the noise enveloped us like a hot, curry-scented blanket, I realized the ambient sound would drown our words out, blocking any potential eavesdroppers.

The moment we had our trays and sat nestled at a table in the corner, Carden tangled his fingers with mine. "You know I'd follow you to the ends of the earth."

I was not in the mood for his charms and untangled my fingers from his. "Not now."

He looked taken aback. I'd never had any qualms about giving my tongue free rein, and yet I'd never spoken to Carden like *this*.

But the issue was too important. I knew where my mother was. I grew up thinking she'd been a Florida housewife who'd died young. But not only was she alive, she was a part of my messed-up world. The coincidence was exhilarating. Overwhelming.

Had *Ronan* known? Because my recruitment couldn't have been a coincidence.

That my biological mother and I had both been found and imprisoned by these vampires—it was the biggest connection ever. We both, somehow, through our choices, had found ourselves in the darkest place in the world.

All the clichés suddenly felt true. I truly was my mother's daughter. And I had to save her. No matter what. At all costs. Period.

"Fine, lass. I'm listening. Why the sudden urgency?"

I told him. I had no choice. I confessed everything.

Well, not *everything*. I think he'd probably kill Ronan with his bare hands if he knew we'd kissed. And I would keep Ronan's counsel and remain silent about the truth behind the misericordia and his involvement. But I had to tell Carden about Dagursson, about his relationship with Charlotte.

About how members of the Synod were now holed up in some stronghold in Norway, where they were holding my mother hostage. Charlotte was going to find them—not to rescue my mother, but so she could have the pleasure of killing her in front of me.

I told him. And then silence.

"Carden?" He wasn't jumping into action the way I'd hoped he would. Charlotte had implied he was the one lying. But surely he hadn't known *this*. "Did you know that about my mom? You didn't, right?"

I tried to catch his eye to gauge what was going on in his

head, but he was too busy staring at my tray. "You going to eat that...that disc?"

"This?" I speared said disc onto my fork. "Yeah, Salisbury steak." I bit off a chunk, eager to eat and run. Speaking as I chewed, I detailed the plan. "I spoke with Tom, and he said he can get us on a boat to the Shetlands."

"Us?" Carden was eyeing me like I'd begun speaking Greek. "Tom?"

"The Draug Keeper. That Tom." As I cut my meat into smaller chunks, I elaborated, "From the Shetlands, we'll catch a floatplane to Reykjavik. Then onto a cargo ship to Hammerfest, Norway. Fun fact: Nazis took over Hammerfest during World War II. I guess there must've been some vamps among them, because they didn't want to leave once the war was over. Those crazy-ass Synod vampires—you know, like Jacob and the ones who held you hostage? Apparently there's a whole nest of his crew nearby." I paused to catch Carden's eye. Was this all news to him? I still couldn't tell. "Just stop me if you know all this already. Anyway, the vampires all live on an industrial island off the coast—it's called Melkøya. Did you know that was such a thing? Industrial islands, I mean? The place is just one big factory. Apparently, it's the endpoint of an undersea gas pipeline."

Did he know this? For all I knew, he'd been to Melkøya before. For all I knew, he'd already seen my mother there.

I took another angry bite of my steak, even though my appetite had fled. The blank look he was giving me made my belly twist. "Do you like the plan?"

"This is no plan. There *is* no plan. Because you're not leaving."

"Of course I'm leaving." I let out a little nervous laugh. My heart was beating double-time now. What was his problem? We were always on the same page about things. What was going on? "I assumed you'd go with me. I mean, hello? My mother is alive and being held prisoner?"

He leaned back from the table, kicking his feet out. "It's too dangerous. It'll be the time of The Rising for those fools."

Hearing his calm statement made my world flip over on itself. "So you...you knew? You know about this island, about everything?"

"Be at ease, lass. I don't know everything. All I know is the Synod holds some fool summit at the advent of every polar night. That's what they'll be about. Travel there is impossible. The reward isn't worth the risk."

"Excuse me? The reward? This isn't some prize—"

His hand whipped out, grabbed my own, and held it almost too tightly. "Do you know why they have your mother? Why they keep her? She is of an ancient and powerful bloodline. Have you ever wondered at your own appeal to the vampires? At your own strength?" I opened my mouth to reply, and he cut me off. "No, it is not because of your innate talents," he scoffed, "much as you'd like to think it."

"No need to be mean," I grumbled.

"This is no time to be peevish, Annelise. There are many talented people on this earth. But your mother, you...you hail from some very powerful ancestors. And to feed from your blood—"

I sat upright, said blood chilling in my veins. "*You* feed from this blood."

Uncertainty scratched at the very recesses of my soul.

His features hardened. "Do you doubt my affections? Don't forget—you fed me first." He softened. "But aye, what you say is true. Your blood holds power, just as *mine* holds power for *you*. And would you say that's the only reason you choose to be with me?"

Would I still choose him without the bond we shared? If there were no blood fever?

Thoughts like that were unproductive. Carden was here, now, with me. I deflated, feeling silly at my momentary spurt of doubt. Now was not the time to go crazy girlfriend on him. "No, you're right. That's not why I'm with you."

"And so you see? You can't go. You'd be in too much danger. Your mother is a prisoner, yes, but she is not in mortal danger. She is too valuable to them alive. As you would be. They would only want to imprison you, too. And your heart is younger than hers. Think what would happen were they to use you to do more than merely feed vampires, but to create them?"

Despair washed over me.

But...my mom.

What was she doing now? Would she recognize me if she saw me? Would we resemble each other? I had to see her. I couldn't bear this. I needed to rescue her from what surely was a fate worse than death.

A handful of Guidons swanned into the dining hall, and I canted my head to the side to avoid being struck by a wayward tray.

"Listen," I told him with renewed intensity, "with you helping me, I'd have a shot, right? You and I could totally save her. Or need I remind you how good I am at rescuing people from Jacob's dungeons?" I nudged him, a reminder that I'd saved *him* from exactly that.

He sat back again, arms crossed with finality. "I cannot allow you to go. Trust me when I say that now is not the right time. I forbid it."

"You forbid it?" I put my fork down and stared at him. I'd had to raise my voice to be heard over the rising din. "Last I checked, I was in charge of my own self, thank you very much."

"Not so long as we're bonded—"

Bonded, bonded, bonded. Wasn't that supposed to make me stronger?

I leaned forward, and my whispered words came out a frustrated hiss. "You said yourself the bond was a partnership. A thing that deepened our relationship. Not something that hobbled me. This isn't the eighteenth century, Carden. I haven't gone off to some man's home never to return to my own. I'm shocked family doesn't mean more to you."

His features hardened in an instant. "Shocked? I'm shocked you'd think yourself capable of so ridiculous a plan. Shocked you'd be so foolish to have faced Dagursson and Charlotte alone in the first place."

"I lived, didn't I?" I was tired of trying to prove I was stronger than what he took me for.

"Aye, and lucky you were indeed. Why didn't you ask me for help? What would I have done if something had happened to you? You, a child, facing two of my kind alone—"

Now he was just making me feel dumb. "I'm not that stupid," I snapped.

The moment the words were out, I knew I'd made a mistake.

He put words to his realization, slowly and coldly. "You weren't alone."

I gave the barest shrug and braced myself.

"Because you were with Ronan," he said. It was a statement, not a question.

I was shaking my head before he finished speaking. "I can explain. Dagursson was going to kill Ronan. I was right there, outside his office. There wasn't time to find you. It all just… happened." I needed to explain this just right, but it was hard to concentrate. The noise from the next table had gotten loud enough to draw my eye away from him. "Can't these people chill for two minutes?"

I scooted around in my chair to see what was going on. My eyes went straight to Regina, despite the fact she was the smallest person in the room. She was like a little black cloud, if clouds were comprised of scowls and nerves. I'd have sworn she had a neon *kick me* sign hanging over her head.

Is that how I looked? Because, yet again, there was something about her that resonated with me. Maybe it was the height thing, her being short like me. Why else had I gone to her defense in the first place? More than that, I'd come to consider her a bit of a protégé. We'd developed a rapport, bolstered in large part by the fact that she was the one who'd come to find me when Ronan was in the process of being slowly killed by the torture-happy Dagursson.

And now the Guidons had descended on Regina and were messing with her in the usual dining hall bullying ways. Sprinkling bread crumbs into her hair. Pulling her tray away again and again, just at the last minute. Slowly drizzling her drink onto her plate, her shoulders.

"I am so sick of this," I murmured. I'd been unable to save Emma or cure Yasuo. And I couldn't rescue my mom right this minute. But I could help Regina. I scooted my chair back and shifted my weight forward, sliding my feet into place. I didn't care what gaffe the poor girl had inadvertently perpetrated, she did not deserve this treatment. "I'm over it."

The weight of Carden's hand on my forearm held me back. "You've done enough to call attention to yourself. Every move you make tempts fate. Now please, love, stop being contrary."

I froze. I was done taking orders.

But then he spoke again, his voice low and cold. "This is not the way to save your mother."

I glanced back at Regina, at the glop of cream soup that'd made a swath of her curls hang flat and beige. "But—"

His fingers tightened into a grip. "You cannot."

My shoulders fell. I was trapped. Trapped in this dining hall. And, as long as I was bonded to a vampire, I was trapped on this island. Trapped in this strange, sadistic world until someone more powerful than me decided otherwise. I forced my muscles to go lax.

This was one time I wouldn't be able to help poor Regina. She was on her own. We all were.

Defeat and anger warred inside me. But I needed to keep my priorities in mind, and right now my only priority was my mother. I dropped back into my seat, mumbling. "What's the saying? Lie back and think of England?"

Carden's expression warmed, a smile curling the edges of his hard mouth. "Never that, lass. She's not *my* queen."

With a heavy sigh, I stole one last glance at the hazing going on at the other table.

I was so sick of these people. Sick of getting hassled. Of watching other kids get hassled. Or worse, seeing how fear turned them into feral and sadistic little tyrants. All in the name of survival of the fittest. "Darwin would've loved this place, I swear."

He chuckled.

The reassuring sound made me turn back around in my seat. I supposed Carden was right. I needed to lie low, which meant I shouldn't get involved.

I pushed the steak around on my plate. Picked up my fork. Put it down again.

"You need nourishment." Carden gently took my hand and wrapped it back around the utensil. "Now tell me why you insist on being so defiant. I have told you your mother is in no immediate danger. We will find her and save her in good time. What put this fool notion into your head, that you might just leave and reunite with her as though you were a normal woman and not what you are?"

What I am? Suddenly my throat was too tight to speak. I wasn't the one knee-deep in half-truths, and yet he spoke to me like I was the troublesome one.

"How can you be so certain about this island dungeon? Ye wee loon, thinking to go off half-cocked."

He was being his casual Carden self, but the dismissive tone made me anxious to explain myself. "Charlotte gave me a list—"

"She wrote you a *list*?" He made it sound like she and I were planning our grocery shopping or something.

"Not like that," I said, on the defensive. "It was a list of numbers."

"Numbers," he repeated.

"Geographic coordinates," I explained. I hadn't given up hope—I still wanted to convince Carden I was in earnest. Because with or without his help, I *would* go forward with my plan. As it was, I was still disheartened I'd been unable to help Regina. I needed to assert some agency in my life—especially when it came to this, my mother, the most important thing. "She said it's the exact location of where my mother is being held. I mean, she might be lying, but—"

Carden's voice hardened. "Have no doubts. When one such as Charlotte wants to trip you up, she will have no trouble doing so."

"Whose side are you on?" I shrugged a shoulder, imagining the cynical sentiment rolling off my back. "Thanks for the vote of confidence, Carden. Seriously, I didn't realize you were such a Charlotte fan." I had to speak loudly to be heard. The noise from the other table was getting louder.

"Ignore them," he said, reading my thoughts.

"Yeah, I'm trying, but—" The sound of hooting boys had joined the din. I flinched from Carden and threw my fork down. Something inside me had cracked for good. "I'm sorry. I can't. She's my friend." I realized the words were true as I spoke them.

I turned, and something crystallized in me, seeing the leggy Guidon who stood behind Regina. Her name was Paige—she'd been a friend of Masha's—and she currently had a fistful of Regina's hair. Paige's weapon was some fancy butterfly knife, and she had mad skills. The blades flicked open and shut, dancing over her knuckles, getting closer and closer to Regina's throat.

I found my feet. Began to stand.

Carden's grip reached me again, and this time it was a vice of steel around my forearm. "I said no. That child needs to find her own way."

Anger boiled up in me—at this place, those girls, my help-lessness, and yes, at Carden, too. I shot him a look, letting the full strength of so many pent-up emotions burst through. "Let me guess. I need to lie low?" An image of Yasuo—the old Yas—slammed into my mind with the force of a blow. I should've fought his transition. I should've fought for Emma, too. I should've fought Charlotte when I had the chance. *Would've. Should've.* "What good is lying low when it keeps getting my friends killed?"

"Softly now, Ann. I'm sorry for your friends, truly I am. But *you* are the only human who concerns me." His eyes held mine, and I felt a strange fog wash over me, like a fuzzy calm suffusing my brain.

Fuzzy and calm. Basically, something *not* me.

I pulled away like I'd been burned. "What was that?" I put a hand to my temple, rubbing where the sensation had been the most acute. "You didn't tell me the bond could do that."

But Carden's gaze had moved from me, aimed at a point over my shoulder. His lips thinned. "Fool. What is he thinking coming here?"

The way my heart thudded to life, I knew whom I'd see when I turned.

Ronan. He hadn't left.

But he wasn't looking at either of us. He was striding across the hall, straight for Guidon Paige. His expression was laser-focused fury.

It was exhilarating.

In typical Ronan fashion, he didn't make a fuss. Didn't bluster or throw his weight around. He placed a palm on Regina's tray and slid it back into place before her. He murmured something.

I strained to listen, but Ronan wasn't one to shout. I imagined his rasping Scottish burr, all the while hating that I couldn't hear.

But I watched the results clearly enough.

Paige was frowning like a kid whose lollipop was just taken, but still, she stalked away. The crowd thinned, boys wandered back to their tables, and girls drifted away in clusters of twos and threes.

Ronan had helped Regina. He'd stopped whatever was going down. Of course he did. Stupid and tender-hearted was just like him.

He lifted his head, and like the opposite pole to my magnet, his eyes came straight to me. Bored into me.

"You're the girl my brother's in love with."

Once again, those remembered words rocked me. The memory of his last stolen kiss pierced into the very core of me.

My breath caught and held until my fingers went tingly, but still he looked at me.

A growl came from beside me. "Reckless pup."

Crap. Carden's eyes had slid to me. And here I was gaping at Ronan like he was the last cupcake at the bakery.

Crap crap crap.

What was wrong with me?

I forced myself to look away. To look to Carden. Who was, by the way, my *boyfriend*. Not to mention an inordinately powerful and immortal vampire who could destroy anyone on this island should the whim strike—me and Ronan included.

"His recklessness will get him killed."

I swallowed hard. "It was just a Guidon," I said, trying my best to sound calm. "You really think it was that reckless?"

His gaze lingered on me, like he knew that I knew that wasn't the only reckless behavior coming from Ronan these days.

"I don't think," Carden said. "I know."

Then something shifted in his expression. Like he'd come to a decision. It unnerved me.

He took my hand, and in the most gallant move ever, turned it and placed a soft kiss on the inside of my wrist. As his lips lingered on my skin, his eyes flicked ever so briefly to Ronan and back again.

Carden might not have said anything else, but his gesture shouted clearly enough: *Mine.*

CHAPTER FOUR

I was so done with this place. Something fundamental had splintered inside me. Nothing was more important than finding my mother alive. Carden thought he could control me, but nobody controlled me but *me*. I would find and help my mom no matter what anyone—human or vampire—said.

So that was it. I'd hoped Carden would help me, but it looked like I was leaving that night—alone.

I thought I had everything I needed, but after tripping in the darkness one too many times on the way to my rendezvous with Tom, I remembered the one thing I could really use.

And so I was crouched in the back of Ronan's Range Rover hunting for his superpowerful LED flashlight when he found me. I'd been thoroughly engrossed, riffling through his kit bag, so I was taken by surprise when his whisper came out of nowhere.

"Ann?"

I jumped back with a squeak, slamming my head against the back window.

"Why are you here?" His tone was curious and soft and—oh God—did he think I'd come to meet him? Were we going to discuss what'd happened between us?

He opened the door wide, and my skin felt hot in the blast of cold air. I felt like I'd just seen him, like we'd just...*done stuff*, but it'd only been my dream.

Focus, focus. Nothing mattered now but saving my mother. Dreams of Ronan were just that—silly, girlish dreams.

I shielded myself from the tenderness I heard in his voice. Whatever feelings there were between us couldn't be. I was leaving this island, leaving *him*. Hunting his sister.

I held up the flashlight like a torch. "Just needed a flashlight."

That was all. Nothing more. *Right?*

His voice honed into a sharp edge, cracking something inside me. "Why?"

Looked like we weren't going to be discussing those kisses. I swallowed hard, then went on the offensive. "Why are *you* here?" I asked evenly. "I thought you were leaving."

"Nice to see you, too." He sighed, and it made him sound so unbearably tired. "It seems I couldn't stay away."

My resolve frayed just a little. It always did when faced with those haunted green eyes. But I needed to blind myself from his concern, from him. "Sorry...I just...what is it, Ronan?"

What do I have that you want?

We'd shared two kisses, but that was it. And those had felt like they'd occurred on a different plane, some unearthly space borne of the life-threatening intensity of the moment. It wasn't like he'd given me any indication that he wanted more. He hadn't gone to Carden afterward, proclaimed his love, demanded a showdown. It wasn't like he wanted *me*.

He had other things on his mind now and so did I. What'd

happened between us was a weird mistake that apparently we were not going to address.

Something had crackled between us, sure, but that'd been before he knew his sister was alive and the island was about to explode with drama. With Charlotte's return and Dagursson's death, there would be power grabs all around. Ronan would be watching his back right now, not thinking about me.

And me, I needed to get out of here. I had a boat to catch.

I crawled forward from the very back, ready to let myself out, but Ronan had slid into the car and quietly clicked the door shut. "I need to know," he said. "Why do you need a flashlight in the middle of the night?"

I debated telling him everything. Carden wouldn't entertain my plan, but Ronan might. He was the one person who kept swooping in to help me.

But Charlotte was his sister. Ronan was happy she was alive. He'd admitted it himself. And I was off to track her to some mysterious island. I'd need to face her. Maybe kill her.

I'd never had a real family, so I couldn't say for sure, but I imagined that when push came to shove, he'd side with her. I'd only just found out where my mother was, and already I was willing to risk everything to save her.

I thought these things, but all I said was, "The batteries in mine died."

I cracked open the door. I needed to go. Even though this was the worst possible goodbye.

His arm swung out; he grabbed the door and shut it. "Uh-huh." My heart thudded as he climbed into the backseat to join me. "And why could this not wait until tomorrow?"

"I..."

"You..." he mimicked. He flopped next to me. Did he have to sit so close? The car practically pulsed with Ronan-ness. I didn't remember the back of this vehicle being so cramped. "How about I answer the question for you. You are being too reckless. Again."

Reckless. It's what Carden had said about him.

My skin flushed hot in the darkness. We were both reckless. It made me feel like we were a pair. A team. There was a connection between us that had nothing to do with any chemical reaction.

With thoughts of Carden, the now-familiar guilt surged back, leaving me queasy and uncertain.

Carden. *He* was my boyfriend. My bonded vampire. What was I even thinking, allowing myself to sit here with Ronan in the dark?

It was all so complicated. But there was one thing that wasn't complicated. Saving my mother.

I needed to get out of the car.

I lifted my hand. Faltered. Dropped it.

I couldn't leave it like this between us. I needed just a few minutes more before goodbye. I hardened my voice against the torrent of emotions. "Me? How about you? You're out, too. What are *you* doing?"

"Midnight swim."

I eyed his buttoned-up peacoat, his jeans and boots. No wet suit in sight. "I don't believe you."

"Does it matter?" There was the slightest hint of despondency in his words. He shifted his head, casting my face into moonlight. "You're still avoiding the question. How'd you even get in here? I thought I'd set the alarm."

My fingers skimmed along the door, finding the latch. I should be opening it to leave. "Breaking and Entering first semester, remember?"

It surprised a laugh out of him, and for a moment I found

myself facing the old Ronan. Something that'd been clenched deep down in my chest unwound.

Ronan. I didn't need a bond to feel seen by him. Appreciated.

It was almost like he sensed what I was feeling because he broke the moment with a jingling of his keys. "Come on, then. I'll take you back. If we're discovered, I'll tell them I had you running a midnight beach circuit."

I snapped out of my stupid reverie and scooted deeper into the shadows. "I'm not going back."

He turned and thoroughly scrutinized me, his gaze raking down my body, sizing me up, assessing my layers of clothing, the extra sweater, my coat and scarf, finally lingering on the bag at my knees, which burst with enough gear to last several days. I was hidden in shadows, and yet every second his eyes were on me felt like a blaze of light, warming me, illuminating my darkest places.

"Where are you going?" he asked finally, and for a second, I imagined he sounded injured.

I numbed myself to the stabbing in my chest. I had a mission, my own mission. I was on my way. I was in a race to save my mother. I was gunning for Charlotte.

I gave a hard nod.

"So, you were just going to leave?" This time there was definitely something in his voice.

"Yes," I said simply.

"With no goodbye?"

Yeah, right. *Bye, I'm off to kill your sister...or be killed by her.*

"Sorry. I have to. But I'm, uh, I'm glad I got to see you..." I tapered off lamely.

His face became a mask, absent of all expression.

What did this tense silence mean? Was he disappointed I

was leaving, or merely disappointed I'd break the rules so flagrantly?

He was waiting for me to say more, but I couldn't reveal anything else. Finally, he spoke again, his voice grown cold. "So you feel you can't trust me enough to tell me what you're about? And to think…"

"To think what?"

"Never mind, Ann." There was that sigh again. "Never mind me."

I felt an invisible wall inserting itself between us. We were each building a dam, holding our emotions away from each other.

I couldn't let him believe I didn't trust him. Sometimes it felt like Ronan was the *only* person in the world I did trust.

"I do trust you," I said finally, unable to bear this tension. "I just can't tell you."

He looked down the beach, right toward what I'd thought was a well-hidden cove, and guessed my intent. "You're going by sea. You're off to meet Tom. Is that it?"

I shifted, uncomfortable all over. It was exactly what I was doing. How did Ronan manage to guess everything about me?

I checked my watch. "I need to go."

Tom had helped girls escape before. He knew me and liked me. I knew he'd help, and sure enough, it'd not taken more than two minutes in his cottage before the old Draug Keeper got a look I knew well. He sucked on his teeth and in a bored voice, had said, "'Bout time you flee this place. I'd flee the vamps if I could."

Fleeing. It was tempting…so tempting. I could *not* believe I wanted to travel to an island with yet more vampires.

Neither could Tom, but he offered to take me in his boat all the same. He'd drop me in Shetland, the first hurdle in this deadly race with Charlotte.

"You didn't answer my question," Ronan said. "Is Tom the one helping you?" He waited patiently, his attention unwavering. He had that ability, comfort in uncomfortable silences. He'd wait forever for me to speak next if he had to.

I wonder what else he'd wait for.

I shook the thought from my head.

"If you say so," I replied, even though I knew the comment would annoy him. I had to get rid of him. The clock was ticking. I *had* to go. I didn't know why I was even still sitting there, but I was trapped in a web, and Ronan was one very large, very handsome spider.

His expression hardened, suddenly suffused with some carefully controlled emotion. "Does *he* know where you're going?"

"Tom?"

He hissed. "Och, Ann, you know who I mean. *Him*. Carden."

I squirmed with the knowledge that whatever I said next was of unutterable importance. The truth might cut him in a way I never would've intended. "Didn't you want to ask more about Tom?"

Once more, his face became a careful blank. "So he does know." Another protracted silence filled the car. Tension thrummed through me as Ronan studied the beach, studied my gear. Studied me. "And yet he's not here. Are you finally fleeing the vampires and escaping this godforsaken isle?"

It wasn't the direction I'd expected this conversation to go, and I let out a humorless laugh. "Would you stop me?"

"Stop you?" He took my hand in his. Suddenly the old Ronan was back, and the force of his presence, his attention, took my breath. "Ann, I'd help you. Why did you not trust enough to tell me? You wee fool, were you afraid of telling me? You know I'm more than just your teacher. How could you not know that? How could you not think I'd want to help you? Getting off this island to safety is all I've wanted for you."

His intensity, the sudden earnest yearning I saw in his eyes, flashed me to my last conversation with Carden. Why wasn't my vampire trying to get me off the island to safety?

Stop. I needed to stop that sort of thinking.

"Tell me." He held my hand so firmly in both of his, a thumb making circles on my wrist. "How can I help? Where are you going?"

I hated this lie that had unexpectedly sprouted between us. But it was a blessing, too; I didn't see any other way to handle it. I couldn't let Ronan know I was hunting his sister.

I blotted the emotion from my face. "I'm going to Norway."

Ronan laughed.

I snatched my hand away. "Why is everyone laughing at me today?"

That stopped him. "I'm not laughing." He stared at me for a long moment. "Never. I'm just...I confess, I'm so relieved, Ann. Why Norway?"

How can I explain this while leaving Charlotte out of it? I decided the best lies contained a whiff of truth. "I have reason to believe that is where I'll find my...my mother."

His eyes bulged. "Your mother?"

Relief swept me. Part of me had feared he'd known about her imprisonment and kept it from me, too. "So I hear."

I was too busy chanting *don't ask how I know* in my head that it took a moment for his next words to register.

"I'll go with you," he said, and I felt the longing behind the statement like a wave, hitting me, threatening to engulf me. "I'll help you. We'll run together."

He did care about me. Slow, searing, stubborn pain unfurled in my chest. He cared, but this had to be goodbye.

"You can't." Lies. I needed more lies. "There's, um, no room in the boat."

I couldn't pit Ronan against his sister. I was on my own path now.

Would I ever see him again? I couldn't just flee the island and then come back when everything was over. Accepting this felt like being gutted with a dull, rusty blade.

"So, Carden? He's traveling with you then?" He'd tried to act casual, but something in his voice sounded dejected.

His vulnerability cracked me wide open. I dared meet those green eyes. "No. It's just me—"

He turned, practically jumping into action. "Then let me get my things."

I grabbed his arm. I was off chasing *his* sister, and I'd do whatever it took to stop her. *Whatever* it took. "I said no."

How I longed to confide in him. But there was no way I could tell him what I was really doing. How would I even broach it? *Hey, looks like your sister's on a murderous rampage that'll end with you if she thinks I care about you, so how about we go find her and see what happens?*

No way. I'd never ask him to hunt his sister. And I'd never put him in that sort of danger. If Charlotte wanted to kill everyone who was dear to me, I needed to distance myself.

"I need to be alone for this."

"You're not alone, Ann." He took my shoulders in his hands, pulling me to face him. "Wherever you go, I'll find you."

I tried to wriggle free. This was too hard. The hardest thing I'd ever done. But I had to remind myself that I had a mother, and I needed to find her. My duty was to her. "You can't."

His jaw was tight, eyes glittering in the darkness. "And you can't stop me."

I shored up every bit of strength I had. This had to be goodbye. I had family, Ronan had family, and I could never let the two meet. "Please. Just...don't."

He gazed at me, but he didn't question. Ronan wouldn't.

Something in his gaze faded. His grip eased. "As you wish," he said finally.

"You can't come," I repeated. "But..." For the millionth time since I'd had the dream, my mind returned to it.

"But?" Hope blazed again in his eyes, at once.

It made me say something I knew I might regret. "But... there might be something you can do for me."

CHAPTER FIVE

"Anything," he said quickly. Too quickly. "I'll do anything to help you."

I had to turn away from the intensity. Instead, I gazed out the window. The time of the dimming had begun, and the moon hung large and low, cutting a blade of muted light across the water in the distance. Clouds glowed dark gray in the black sky.

Ronan *thought* he'd do anything. But would he be so quick to pledge loyalty if he knew who I was running off to kill?

Still, I knew he'd jump at the chance to do what I was about to ask: for him to break my bond with Carden.

I'd lied to Ronan—he thought I was going to escape. And maybe a part of me was. Because wouldn't breaking the bond with Carden be exactly that? An escape?

Carden hadn't wanted to hear my plan, hadn't wanted to leave the island. He'd said it was to protect me, but had he wanted to stay for another reason? Because when he couldn't convince me, he'd tried simply to numb the thoughts of going in my head.

But I had to save my mother. Which meant breaking this chemical dependence on my vampire.

If I could sever our bond, I'd be free to make my own choices. Free from everyone's lies and manipulation. Most of all, breaking my bond with Carden would give me the distance to see our relationship for what it truly was.

My mother was out there somewhere, imprisoned by vampires who kept her alive for the richness of her blood. I'd find her and save her, and we'd escape this hell for real.

Maybe Carden did truly love me. But if I couldn't convince him to leave with me, to help me, then I'd not have him bound to me.

"Well?" Ronan's voice was low in my ear.

Finally, I turned back to him, and the look that awaited me was too earnest to bear. I tried not to think how I didn't deserve this loyalty. This ferocity.

I cleared my throat. "I had a dream," I began, and I told him about it. Not *all* of it, but how I'd dreamed about him using his hypnotic touch to quell my blood fever.

I think he must've sensed the rest, though, because by the time I finished talking, he had a wicked glint in his eyes. "So, in your dream, *I touched you*?"

I was used to wicked glints from Carden. But from Ronan? I was practically undone.

I shifted away. How had he gotten so close?

"Yes, you touched me. I mean, with your, you know, your special touch. It was just a dream," I added quickly.

The backseat was shrinking. He was even closer now, close enough to feel the heat of his thigh radiate along mine. His voice was a rasp as he asked, "You dreamed I touched you in a special way?"

Playful—that's all this was. It was Ronan being playful.

This was too dangerous. I needed to part from him. To

push him away. Even if it hurt us both, it'd be an injury so much smaller than the massive and unforgivable sin of killing his sister. Because, if I were to be honest with myself, that was precisely what I was off to do.

"Stop it. Be serious." I shoved him a little, needing to insert space between us. It was a mistake. That chest under his sweater was rock hard. "It was just you using your power. To sever my bond."

His expression froze, and suddenly there was no doubt just how un-playful he was. Ronan was serious. Deadly so. "You're telling me you want to sever your bond with Carden?"

Was that what I was saying?

"I'm saying I want to try. To see what happens."

But as I said the words, I knew I meant every word. Fiercely.

No longer would I be a pawn. I'd be the one moving the pieces on the board. I'd be a player. This was my show. My showdown.

And it began with the bond.

I reveled in the strength in my voice as I said, "It's time for me to be my own woman."

Ronan didn't say anything else. He simply reached for me. Placed a palm on either cheek. He slid his hands down, drawing goose bumps as he slipped them under the collar of my coat. Under my sweater. His fingers quested along my shoulders, thumbs gently sweeping down, until they cradled my collarbones.

Heat unfurled in my chest. Was it his proximity? His warmth? Or was I feeling his powers in action?

"Are you doing it?" I whispered.

He paused, peering deep into my eyes. That damned glint was back in his. "Can you not tell?"

I prayed he couldn't sense the hot blush that'd flooded my

cheeks. Because, apparently, there were no powers yet. This was just what it felt like for me to be touched by Ronan.

I shut my eyes, pretending like I was too deep in concentration to answer. "Just do it."

And *then* I felt it. A humming spread from his palms; it radiated down through my torso and up to the base of my skull. "You don't need him," Ronan whispered. "You are strong."

And I was. I gasped as the sensation overpowered me.

I was strong. I was bulletproof. Invincible.

I hadn't experienced the full brunt of his power since he'd taken me from that Florida parking lot well over a year ago now. Then, I didn't know Ronan, and I certainly didn't know there was such a thing as special powers in this world. At the time, I hadn't realized how much I was fighting him off.

But now, now I did know Ronan. What's more, I trusted him. Cared for him.

Okay, I probably loved him.

It meant I opened myself up to him, let myself be vulnerable. And it made me more susceptible to his powers.

"You are separate," he murmured. "Solitary."

I felt a tearing. A ripping through the very heart of me. Blackness and despair swept me, made me dizzy. A cavern of solitude and emptiness bored through my chest.

His fingers curled into me, and the pain grounded me. "Focus," he barked. "You are separate. You do not need."

But I did. I needed.

"You are complete," he intoned. "You do not need any vampire."

I swayed into him.

Ronan. I needed Ronan.

"No," a hoarse rasp tore from him. His fingers curled onto me, as if he might keep hold of me even as he was letting me go. "There is nobody you need, Annelise. You are self-reliance. You are strength, alone."

In that moment, I knew how much strength it took for him to say those words. To let me go.

The loss was almost too much to bear.

For an instant, I was bereft. So bereft. All was darkness and loss.

But then he whispered, "You are strong. You are capable. You are loved."

Power infused me. Lit me from within.

I was loved.

"You do not thirst," he told me, and as he spoke the words I felt as though sweet, cool water filled me. It soaked into the dry cracks of my soul. Infused me, quenched me. Till my belly felt full to bursting.

Ronan's hands slid up, fingers tangling in the hair at the base of my skull. "You are free."

There was pounding on the window. The creak of metal. And a harsh Scottish growl tore me from my reverie. "Just what in bloody hell do you think you're doing?"

CHAPTER SIX

I sprang from Ronan, slamming my head on the window again. "Carden?"

Normally, I always knew when he was near. For so long, he'd been a constant presence on the edge of my consciousness. I opened myself to him now, reaching out with my senses.

I couldn't feel him.

And he looked angry.

"What have you done?" he growled, peering in at us.

I flinched back, and this time I smacked my elbow on the door. "Jeez, this stupid car."

I was being suffocated by maleness all around, so finally I opened the door and spilled out.

Ronan followed right behind me, and I had to step between him and Carden to stop the vampire from throttling the Tracer.

"Don't be mad," I quickly told him. "I can explain."

My heart was hammering, pumping heat into my cheeks. It was from surprise, yes, but guilt, too. Apparently it had become my natural state.

I threw my senses wide, trying to feel if I was in danger, but all I felt was dead air. Carden was a blank to me.

The bond was gone.

"*We* can explain," Ronan said steadily. I felt him step forward to stand close behind me. He placed his hands atop my shoulders. Did he feel the need to protect me?

Carden's eyes narrowed on him. "Get away from my Annelise before I tear your arms off."

But Ronan only held on tighter. "*Your* Annelise?"

"Shut it, pup. You were supposed to be gone for good."

I pulled away and spun around to look at the Tracer. Me fleeing without saying goodbye was one thing, but Ronan? Had his plan been to go and never come back? It slashed to my core. "You're leaving for good?"

He ignored me, though, keeping his eyes steady on Carden. "Ann doesn't belong to you."

"Aye, she does." He bared his fangs as he hissed, "The lass is mine."

I was *his?* They were both discussing me like I was some sort of object to be owned and controlled. My panic flipped into anger. "Hang on one second—"

But Carden spoke over me, his entire focus on Ronan. Like I no longer existed. "What did you do to her?"

Ronan didn't back down. Instead, he shifted me aside and took an aggressive step toward the Vampire. "What you should've done long ago."

"I can explain." I tried to shove my way between them. "I thought—"

"It was not your decision to make," Carden growled at Ronan.

I cleared my throat. "Right, it was mine, and I think I do have some—"

"She needed my help," Ronan snarled back. "An occurrence that's happened once too often. And now she's escaping."

Could vampires get paler? Because it seemed Carden just did.

The corner of Ronan's mouth curled. "And you didn't know." He was loving this.

Not me. I wasn't loving it. At all. While these guys were posturing, my mother was out there languishing in some dungeon.

"You'd have some clue if you weren't so caught up in politics," Ronan added. "But it's always been so for you, hasn't it? It's all about the cause. The cause over all things. You may love Ann, but you love your honor more."

Carden eyed my pack. It'd spilled from the car behind me. "Aye, I love the lass. Enough to know she's not really escaping." It was Carden's turn to smile. "We're just off on a merry race with your sister."

We're. So he was going with me?

It was an evil way to break the news to Ronan, and I couldn't decide how I felt about it. I could definitely use Carden's help, but was he helping me because it was what he wanted, or simply to get the better of Ronan?

"My *sister*?" Ronan's voice was like ice. He turned to me. "What does he mean?"

Crap. Here we go. I let attitude be my armor. "Oh, I'm allowed to speak?"

I needed to separate from Ronan. A small hurt now was safer than a bigger hurt down the road.

"I'm waiting." Ronan's face was an unreadable blank.

"It was your sister who told me where to find my mother."

"Charlotte," Ronan said like he was trying to make sense of it all. "You spoke to Charlotte?"

"Aye," Carden answered with a grin. "Charlotte. And wee Drew wants to stake her. You'd have some clue," he added in a mockery of Ronan's earlier words, "if you weren't so caught up in your puppy crush."

"Enough. Both of you. Enough. Enough." I turned to Ronan. "Yes, your sister came to me. Did you know she killed Emma?"

The slight widening of his eyes, the way they deadened just the tiniest bit, told me he hadn't.

I tried to soften my voice as I finished, "Yeah, well, and then she killed Yas. Right in front of me. Which she must've enjoyed because now she's got it in her head that she'd like me to watch as she kills my mother." So much for the sympathetic voice-softening. I scrubbed a hand over my face. "Look, I just want to find my mom. To save her. Nobody said anything about staking." I shot Carden a look. "I don't know what will happen."

Carden snarled at my back. "Which is precisely why it was an idiotic idea to tamper with our bond. But why would I expect more from—"

I spun to face the vampire. "Severing our connection wasn't Ronan's idea, it was mine. I'm leaving this island, and I don't know what's in store. What I do know is that I need to break the bond if I'm going to think about any of this clearly."

"Your idea." Carden's expression cracked. "Is that true? You wish to break from me?"

An unexpected surge of nostalgia and affection swelled in me. Maybe our relationship wasn't just a chemical bond after all.

"I want to see what it's like to be with you," I said, my voice growing softer, "without the bond. I need to be free to do what I need to do."

"What you need to do?" Carden gave a gruff nod toward Ronan. "Or who?"

I smacked him in the chest. "No, dummy. I just—" I shrugged, looking for the right words "—I don't want to worry that I'll somehow be crippled if I'm ever without you. I need to be able to part from you every once in a while. To know that if I go back to you it's because I want to, not because I'm some sort of addict who has to."

"But you *will* be crippled. You'll be weaker without the bond. Without me." Carden's tone had gone impossibly gentle.

Not Ronan's, though. His next words cracked like a whip, sharp and biting. "She doesn't need your blood to make her strong. Ann is strong on her own. Strong alone."

Carden smirked as he slowly turned to face Ronan. "You just hate that she's been strong without you. That's why you broke the bond. You want to be the one to ride in and save her." His smirk turned into a laugh. "Is that how you think it'll be, ye sodding whelp? You break our bond, and surprise, Annelise needs you again, right on schedule?"

Suspicion smacked me, full force. The way Carden discussed our broken bond—he wasn't baffled, surprised, or confused.

"You knew," I said, and something in my voice startled him enough to pull his attention from Ronan. "You knew Ronan could break the bond. You let me think it was permanent. Forever."

Carden was by my side in an instant, his finger gently tilting my chin up. "And so I'd have it. I'd have you bonded to me for an eternity."

Ronan grunted dismissively, and Carden shot him a quelling look.

"Eternity," I said uneasily. "I'd have to be a vampire for that."

He gave me a grave nod. "The day might come when you choose such a fate."

An involuntary shiver crawled up my spine. *Be one of the undead?* Not that. Never that.

The prospect filled me with revulsion. And just what did that say about my feelings for my boyfriend?

I shook my head. I needed to face one issue at a time. "That day isn't here yet," I said firmly. "Either way, I don't want to be chemically attached to my boyfriend. Breaking the bond isn't the same as breaking up."

Ronan stiffened. "It's not?" he muttered under his breath.

More guilt. I was swamped with it. Would it ever stop?

I forced myself to keep going. To not look at Ronan. I needed to insert space between us. Because, if I did have to kill his sister, he'd never forgive me, and that was something I couldn't bear. I needed to be away from him when I faced her. Away from him for the aftermath. Away.

Ronan meant a lot to me—so much—but he was all unplumbed depths. He represented a bellyful of butterflies and decisions made with little thought and great consequence. Ronan was mystery and silence, and secret, scorching kisses.

Whereas Carden was, well, he was my boyfriend, if a vampire could be such a thing. We'd shared so much, he'd given me *so much*, not least of all his love and support. I owed it to him—to us—to give this relationship a shot. And if we did end up parting someday, it had to be because of me, my choices, not because someone or something was muddling my head.

It was time to see how I was...what this was...without the bond. How I felt without it. Who I was. What I wanted.

I slid my hand into Carden's. "I'm still with you. We're just no longer...you know, chemically linked."

The vampire glared at Ronan. "But make no mistake. We're linked in other ways. As you'd be wise to remember."

I elbowed him. "Easy, cowboy."

But Carden wasn't done. He wrapped his arm tightly around me and said, "I don't need a bond to be close with my wee dove."

Ronan stared blindly at the vampire's arm around my shoulder, and the defeat in his eyes broke something inside me. I willed him to look at me instead. I wanted to communicate something to him. Remind him of the connection we shared—Ronan might not have been my boyfriend, but he was, I realized, my best friend.

After a long moment, he finally looked up, but he met Carden's eyes instead of mine. "It's always easy for you, isn't it? It's always been easy."

With a grin, Carden tugged me closer. "With the birds, you mean?"

I groaned and tugged away. "Give it a rest, would you? My mom is locked in a dungeon somewhere. I don't have time for testosterone. I need to get out of here."

"Actually," Ronan said, "I'll be going with you after all. It's time for me to have a chat with my sister."

"Och, pup, there's where you're wrong. You won't be with us. Freya orders that you go to her. Now."

I looked from one to the other, fighting a childish twinge of jealousy. "Freya?"

"You could say she's our queen," Carden explained. "We serve her in the fight to take down the Directorate."

I looked to Ronan. He'd told me about this before, though he'd never mentioned any vampire queen. "She's Sonja's sister," he said simply.

I fought back a chill. "Sonja has a *sister*?"

"She's the one who ordered Dagursson killed," Ronan told

me, and the scolding look Carden shot his way gave me pause. "And now she'll have to wait a bit longer for me."

"You dare not disobey," Carden said through gritted teeth.

A charged and silent stare hung between the two men.

I couldn't bear it any longer. "This is about my mom, remember? Not some pissing match between you two. Now if you'll excuse me, I need to get out of here before another minute passes."

Carden grinned. "Aye, then let's be off, love. I find myself eager for the sea breeze on my face."

I felt Ronan deflate. Something inside me dimmed in response.

"Let's just go," I told Carden quietly. I needed to get him out of there before his possessive boyfriend bit got any more extreme.

Despite our lost bond, Carden must've sensed my sadness, because he surprised me by saying, "You two have your good-bye." He gave a brisk nod to me and Ronan. "I must go and get my things. 'Twill be a long, cold journey. My wee dove will be in need of my woolen plaid."

He just had to get in one last stab. Was it love that had him so ragingly possessive? Or just the desire not to let someone else win?

Before I could address the adolescent remark, Carden turned and headed back up the path.

I braced myself, afraid of what I'd see when I turned to Ronan. But I summoned my courage and faced him.

He didn't seem angry. Just...sad.

That was way worse.

"I'm so sorry about Emma and Yasuo. I'd hoped..." His sigh made him sound about a thousand years old and made me wish I could pull him close one last time. "Well, it no longer matters." He defaulted to teacher mode and looked down at my boots, where he'd know my throwing stars would be hidden. "You have your shuriken?"

I nodded tightly, studying my feet. I didn't trust my voice.

Would I have to face his sister? Would I survive it? Would this be our last goodbye?

"Ann," he whispered. He tipped a finger under my chin to raise my eyes to his. "If it's Jacob who's holding your mother, you will be facing many dangers. You've your stakes, too?"

I nodded again, throat clenched with a flood of memories. Of the first time I'd seen his hidden stakes…and his bare chest. He'd stripped off his sweater, then his shirt, to tear fabric to bind my injured ribs.

"Yeah," I managed, my voice tight. "It's the best thing you've showed me." I wasn't sure if I'd wanted that to be as suggestive as it'd come out, but somehow suggestive undercurrents had become standard in my every exchange with Ronan.

He gave me a quiet smile, like he knew what I was thinking. The smile faded quickly, though. "Are you sure of this? Because once you run from this isle, everything changes."

I had no choice. "It's my mom," I said quietly. "My actual mom."

I could see he knew. He understood. Of course he did. It was Ronan—he understood better than anyone. "And you're sure…you're sure you don't need me?"

He was asking a thousand different things with one question. It was too much. I wasn't ready for goodbye. But I had no choice. I tried to smile it off. "Ronan, you know I always need you."

His eyes glittered in the moonlight. "It's no joke. You're setting onto a dangerous path. Leaving like this…life will never be the same for you."

I attempted a laugh. "Thank God."

He gripped my upper arms. "Truly, Ann. Alcántara will be furious. And, despite your successes, it's quite possible Headmaster Fournier will not allow you back. All of it will be different."

There was a sharp twinge in my chest. All of it? My voice cracked as I dared ask, "And you?"

"And I?" He clutched me to him then and wrapped me in his arms. "For you, I am unchanging." Just as I let myself melt into him, clawing the back of his coat like I might never let go, he pushed me away. "You don't want my help with this, and I must accept that. I don't know what you'll find when you get where you're going." His focus on me grew intense. "But remember: fear is your greatest weapon."

"Being afraid?"

He shook his head. "Making others so. Just as fear is your greatest danger, so too is it your most powerful weapon." He glanced around, making sure Carden was gone. The misericordia appeared in his hands.

He dipped to his knees, and I gasped as his hands slid along my leg. He slipped the ceremonial blade deep into my right boot, nestling it next to a stake I'd also hidden there.

His touch buzzed with warmth even through layers of fabric. My skin pulsed in its wake, the blade such a physical reminder of how we were in this together. How we had secrets and how we'd keep them, even when parted by an impossibly wide sea.

"Are you sure?" I whispered, afraid even to speak about such a powerful weapon. "I thought you were going to get rid of it."

"It's too valuable." He stood and took my hand in his, as though the blade weren't the only valuable thing he was discussing. "You must keep it hidden. Even from Carden.

Vampires—*all* vampires—desire this weapon above all others. You must not let anyone disarm you of it."

Anyone. Was he thinking of his sister? Would he realize how I might use this to face her? And yet he was surrendering it to me.

"The misericordia represents unbounded power," Ronan said. "A vampire, any vampire, would do anything to have it for their own."

And he had borne this burden for me. He'd risked so much for me. Continued to do so.

"Thank you," I said, but it wasn't nearly enough.

"Keep it safe, and it will keep you safe. There might come a moment when your life hangs in the balance. If there is no other choice, if you wield this blade, you must do so swiftly and with confidence. The misericordia is the only thing that will make a Vampire feel true fear."

A humorless chuff of breath escaped me. I wriggled my ankle, feeling the weight of the weapon against my calf. "Now you're making *me* scared, Ronan."

He cupped my cheeks. "Just...survive."

"I always do." I was afraid he might kiss me again. I was afraid that, this time, I wouldn't be able to stop.

Ronan's gruff voice broke the tense silence. "Where are you going? Tell me. I want to know."

"I...I can't say." I couldn't have him follow me. I couldn't mess this up. I needed to save my mother, and who knew how Ronan's presence would affect his sister's actions?

"Ann? I meant what I said."

"About?"

"I will find you. I will always find you."

I pulled back ever so slightly. I saw in his eyes just how deadly serious he was. Too serious.

I tried to lighten the mood by saying, "Of course. You're a Tracer, right? It's your job."

He didn't crack a smile. Once again, he was completely unknowable to me. Unreadable.

I didn't know what I had with Ronan, nor did I know what I would find once I left. All I knew was that Carden was still my boyfriend. I cared about him. I *adored* the guy.

I needed to be fair. I had to give him a chance.

My voice was tight as I said simply, "Goodbye, Ronan."

CHAPTER SEVEN

I wasn't even halfway down the rutted path to the beach when a hand clamped over my mouth. Instinct was always only a hairsbreadth away, and my body exploded to life until I was wriggling like a lunatic.

"Surprise," a male voice whispered in my ear. There was something familiar about it, and yet there was a slight lisp I couldn't place.

I fought the urge to panic and flail, and went still instead. *Stay calm. Assess.*

"I've been looking forward to this." His breath was hot and smelled like curry fries, what they'd served earlier in the dining hall. Definitely human, then. Not vampire. A Trainee.

I didn't have time for this.

I tapped into my anger, always carried so close to the surface now. The familiar fury washed over me, energizing me. I could face Trainees in my sleep.

"Not as much as I have." I angled my body to the side as I yanked his wrist tighter across my body. The move was counterintuitive, but it created a small pocket of space under his armpit. Gripping his wrist, I ducked and was free. With a spin, I wrenched his arm behind his back. "You boys should know by now it takes more than—" I finally realized who I was fighting. "Jeez! Rob! I thought you were…"

I was so startled I almost let go, but months of training kept my fingers curled tightly into his flesh.

"You thought I was dead?" He paused in his struggle to look over his shoulder at me. The last time I'd seen him, he'd been left for dead after having his face smashed repeatedly against a fencepost by Yasuo. It finished what I'd started when I'd knocked out one of his fangs. "I'm waiting for you to go first."

I felt energy surge through his body as he readied another attack, but I was prepared. And honestly, I was probably stronger. His face was still a mangled mess. He was shaky, his eyes shifty. He'd consumed too much blood, I suspected, in an effort to heal. Though how—or what—he drank with just the one fang was something I didn't want to consider.

I still had him from behind, and as his muscles tensed, I gave a sharp twist to his wrist. I kicked the back of one of his legs, and he toppled—knees, chest, face—onto the sand. He grunted and turned his head to spit out a mouthful of grit.

I nodded to his misshapen jawline. "What unsuspecting creature did you need to drink to fix that? Because I can't decide if it was enough or way too much."

I was getting cocky, and so I didn't hear the other Trainee approach at my back until rough fingers speared through my hair, scraping my scalp as they seized a handful. "Rob, you're such a fuckup."

The hand wrenched my neck back.

Josh.

Betrayal stole my breath, gutting me.

"Josh?" I pulled free but fell onto my butt, feeling the *plip-*

plip of hairs as they were torn from my scalp. But the pain barely registered. "What is this?"

My heart thudded back to life as two truths became instantly clear. I'd thought Josh was a friend, but I could see by the joyful menace on his face that he really wasn't. And, more pressing, Josh was strong—easily stronger than me.

A grin spread across his beach-bum handsome face. "Happy to see me?"

There was a time when I would've been.

I crab-walked backward, trying to wrap my mind around this latest betrayal. Though really, the seed of doubt had been planted long ago when he'd forged an association with Lilac, my old roommate and nemesis. And later, even more so, when I'd watched him participate in a sick ritual in the heart of the vampires' keep. Now my worst fears were being realized.

He was someone else's ally, not mine.

I forced my heart to harden against this new worldview. "You boys are just full of surprises," I said, silently cursing the crack in my voice. I didn't know how much more hardening my heart could take in this world.

He swiped out a hand to grab me, and I dodged him, finally back on my game. "I thought we were friends," I said, my voice louder now. "What did I do to you?"

Hell, what did I do to anybody to deserve any of this madness?

"We saw Tom readying his boat." Josh's Australian accent lilted the sentence into a question. "Headmaster thought it meant someone might be wanting to make an escape, and it looks like that someone was you. We can't let you do that, can we?"

I popped to my feet and dusted off my hands. He wanted a fight? Fine, I'd give him one. "And you think you can stop me?"

I glanced from him to Rob, who was staring slack-jawed

and one-fanged at Josh with unconcealed worship. "You and who, Hermie the dentist here?"

Rob didn't like that one bit, and his face tightened into a glare of total hatred. "If you think you can just walk off this island, you've got another thing coming."

"I'm not going to walk," I said with all the bravado I could muster. "All *I've* got coming to me is a boat, taking me away from this freak show." I'd just have to make it look like I knocked Tom out and stolen it. The last thing I wanted was for the kindly old Draug Keeper to get in trouble on my account.

I summoned my courage and began to stride back down the path. It was a desperate gamble, but I was out of choices. I could only hope Carden was out there somewhere, on his way to me.

A third Trainee appeared at the top of the ridge. "Dude, I told you guys to wait." He hopped down and popped his knuckles, staring at me like I was a present under his Christmas tree.

I sized him up. The guy was pretty average looking, but I knew better than anyone that looks could be deceiving. For all I knew, he might've been an MMA champion in his former life.

"Hey. Brian, right?" I spoke as calmly as possible. Meanwhile, I was frantically assessing my situation. "What's up?"

I realized the moment it came out that it was a rookie thing to say. Sure enough, he grabbed his crotch. "I'll show you what's up."

I had a sassy reply to that, but it stuck in my throat as they closed in.

There was an explosion of limbs—mine, theirs. Mostly theirs. Josh had gotten behind me and was tying my arms behind my back.

Rob skittered closer, kicking at my ankles, trying to hook my feet. His mouth was a tightly grinning line, his lips molded unevenly, grotesquely, over the gaping hole where his left fang should've been.

I hopped away, but Brian was there to give me a shove. "Careful," he taunted.

Josh shoved me from behind just as Rob kicked again.

I lost my balance and toppled.

I was in the dirt and they were over me in an instant, Josh holding my shoulders, Brian and Rob each holding a leg.

I tried to swallow to get some moisture in my suddenly dry mouth. I held very, very still. I wanted to fight them, but I also didn't want them to find the misericordia tucked into my boot.

"What do you think you're doing?" I demanded, but they weren't listening. And I hadn't needed to ask anyway. Rob had tried having his way with me before, and now he was directing the others to pin my shoulders, to hold an ankle. To move aside.

"I see what this is about," I said, trying to use my sultriest *Hey, boys* voice. "Why don't you free my hands? You know, so I can have free range of movement."

It was worth a shot. I'd say anything to get my hands free.

"We're not that stupid," Brian said.

"Though I know you think we are," Rob said. "You think you're so smart. But who's the one tied?"

"Technically I'm bound, not tied, but whatever you say, Einstein."

His hand shot out before I could grit my teeth, smacking me hard upside my head. My ears started ringing and my mouth filled with the sharp taste of my own blood.

I stilled for a second, just long enough to come to terms with the fact that I was *not* going down this way. Sure, I'd go down eventually in my life, but I'd go fighting.

A hand slithering up my left thigh shocked me into action.

Instinctively, I kicked. My foot connected with Brian's chin.

As he fell back, Rob had to readjust, twisting sideways to try to grab and still my legs. I kicked again, and my heel caught the soft part of Rob's throat. The contact lit me like a lightning bolt, my every nerve igniting.

"Hold her," Brian shouted up at Josh.

Flexing my arms against my restraints, I became a wild thing, my abs working overtime as my feet flailed, legs bucking and thrusting for whatever body part I could connect with.

"I am," Josh snarled. "You hold her. There are two of you."

What I really needed were my weapons, still tucked in my boot. I practically felt the misericordia pulsing at my calf. Beckoning. My hands were behind my back, grinding into the dirt, but if I could reach down low enough and scoot my heel high enough…

If I could reach the blade, I'd be able to flick my wrist and slice through whatever Josh had tied me with. And then…and then the thought of what could happen next was enough to make me light-headed. I'd seen what the ancient blade had done to someone as powerful as Master Alrik Dagursson. What might it do to a few measly Trainees?

I was dying to find out.

I heard myself making crazy banshee noises as I pumped my legs out again and again like a piston, trying to propel Rob and Brian far enough from my feet to tuck my knees and snatch the blade from my boot.

But I was outnumbered, and Rob and Brian worked together to snatch my ankles while Josh kept a death grip on my shoulders, and in a moment, both my feet were pinned.

Rob grinned, briefly forgetting about his missing fang. "Gotcha."

I was still in the fight, though, writhing beneath them. I *needed* my weapons. I would have them.

"Mediocrity," I said, with a nod toward Brian.

He gaped at me like he didn't understand the word. "What?"

"Mediocrity," I repeated, trying desperately to modulate the frantic pitch of my voice. "The state of being mediocre. Or, you know, average. Because this"—I turned my ankle and twisted free of his grip, then swept my leg sideways in a crazy roundhouse kick that clocked him in his jaw—"this is what average gets you."

His chin jerked sideways and he stumbled backward, giving me just enough of a window to tuck my leg. Rob still had my other ankle pinned, and I strained against his hands, tucking myself as tightly as I could, tight enough to feel the individual tissues in my abdominal muscles shredding.

And still, my hands couldn't reach my boot.

"You reaching for your stars?" Brian was wiping his mouth, leaning back toward me. He shoved Rob aside and crawled between my legs. "I guess you're a bitch *and* an idiot, because the laws of physics tell me that you can't do jack while you're tied like that."

I wrenched my shoulder in one last thrust, felt a small pop, and plunged my fingertips into the top of my boot. I felt the cold steel of the misericordia waiting for me. Cold as death, calling me, as though the metal sang a song only I could hear.

I strained to get purchase. "Not physics. Geometry. Angles, dipshit."

I fantasized where I would plunge the misericordia first. The average neck of one average Trainee was in definite danger.

My fingertips swept the butt of the blade. Almost there.

But then Rob dove onto my leg, and I'd have sworn he tore my groin muscle wrenching me flat. "Don't let her."

Brian looked outraged. "What's your problem? Dude, she's *tied.*"

"Yeah," Josh chimed in. "She's just an Acari."

That so? I was done taking crap from these guys.

"She can't do—"

I torqued my foot inward and clenched, freeing my leg. In a single fluid motion, I wrenched my thigh over Brian's shoulder, knocking him off-kilter, and slung one foot, then another over his shoulders, hooking my ankles. I tucked my legs, drawing his head down between my thighs.

"Dude, she wants you," Rob shouted.

My knees were locked tightly, Brian's face in my crotch.

The guys' glee faded the moment they realized what was happening. And then it was too late, because, keeping my ankles hooked, I kicked my legs out hard and snapped his neck.

I kicked my legs until he slid awkwardly onto the dirt, toppling unevenly like the dead weight he was.

"What the fuck?" Rob shrieked. "Did you kill him?" He shot a wild-eyed look to Josh. "Dude, she killed him."

"Wanna go next?" I panted.

"I'll fuck you up." Rob lunged at me, grabbing my face, smashing my cheek into the gravel hard enough for me to feel the tiny rocks slicing into me.

"Fournier said to keep her alive." Josh shoved him away.

"Fine, I'll keep her alive." Rob's cheek ticked as he leveled his eyes on me. "But I'll mess her up first."

I mustered my best smile. "You're messing with the wrong girl."

"You think?" He popped his knuckles.

I couldn't help my eye roll. "Is that supposed to scare me?"

"You're the one pinned. You tell me."

"Rob, let it go." Josh's fingers were like talons digging into my shoulders. "Let's just get on with this."

Rob guffawed. "*Get on this* is more like it." He leaned down and stroked a thumb across my lips.

I snapped my jaw shut, and Rob let out the most satisfying little yelp as I sank my teeth down to the bone. For one glorious second, my eyes met his and I grinned at him around his bloodied thumb.

He smacked me again, harder this time, and it took me a second to get my breath back.

"That all you got?" I managed a bloody smile. "Because, I swear, I will get the best of you."

And then I tensed every muscle in my body as I watched Rob draw back his arm to strike me again.

"Enough," Josh shouted. "It's not your place, Rob. Fournier wants her untouched."

Rob was seething and took a moment to visibly calm his breathing. "Fine. But you play nice," he said to me, "or I'll overrule Josh and take you for a test drive before we bring you in."

I froze at the oddly specific phrase. "In where?"

Josh pulled me to my feet. "It's time for you to visit the keep."

A scream erupted from deep in my gut as I exploded into a violent whirl of kicking and shouldering. I had to escape them. I'd been in the keep before, though the Trainees had no way of knowing that. I'd seen what happened to girls like me. They were drugged and killed, their hearts consumed in a ceremony that was savage and mindless.

I'd watched as my old roommate was stabbed...with the dagger that was now tucked in my boot.

Had the Directorate not noticed the blade was missing? Did they have other weapons like it?

Either way, I was so screwed.

I was outnumbered. Hands confined me. I screamed for Ronan, but he was long gone, and I screamed for Carden, too. But I'd sent him away. I'd broken our bond. Stupid, stupid me. I'd thought independence would make me stronger, but all it meant was my vampire wouldn't feel my panic, my pain.

He'd have no idea I was in trouble.

They held me on either side. A piece of clothing was pulled over my head—someone's old sweater by the smell of it—its sleeves wrapped around my neck to secure it.

I spat damp wool from my mouth as I kicked and writhed. I landed a hit—on Josh, from the sound of it—and I felt a flicker of hope. My bond with Carden might've been broken, but I'd consumed a lot of him in the past months. I was strong.

In one last-ditch attempt at freedom, I tensed my arms, lifting myself from the ground while held in their grip, and flailed with my knees. One foot connected unevenly, and by Rob's grunt, I guessed I'd clipped a groin.

"Hold...still." A hand chopped my back, striking my kidneys dead-on. Damned Josh and his damned med school training.

I bucked again and my feet struck a knee, landing with a sharp crackling snap.

"Fuck this," Josh growled.

Then, a blunt strike on the back of my skull.

Then blackness.

THE NOISE WOKE ME. A tool was slamming rhythmically. Repeatedly.

I tried to open my eyes. Light sliced between my eyelids, and instantly hot tears pooled in my eyes. I squeezed them shut again.

That wasn't any noise; it was merely the throbbing in my head, as though a mallet struck the top of my skull with each heartbeat.

Instinctively, I flexed my abs to get up and get the hell out of there, but was instantly stopped short by leather straps at my chest and feet.

Instant panic dumped adrenaline into my veins, making me flail and thrash, but it was no good. I was restrained.

Oh crap. The misericordia. Had they taken it?

I flexed my ankle, and the bite of that ancient metal felt like acid on my skin. Momentary relief made me woozy. Miraculously, they hadn't found it. I was fully clothed and the blade was still on me, tucked safely where Ronan had hidden it.

I could still feel the heat of his fingers tracing along my leg. Would that be the last time he touched me?

Stop. I had to stop thinking like that.

Ronan couldn't help me in here. He wasn't even allowed inside the keep. And then there was Carden, who refused to enter. So it was just me.

Carden and Ronan would both notice I was gone...only they'd think I was on my way to Norway.

A deep wave of despair overwhelmed me, consuming me with sadness and loneliness so acute it twisted the breath from my chest.

Focus. I needed to focus on my surroundings. Nobody would save me but me.

I knew from my one foray just how vast—and how dangerous—the keep was. There were caverns and areas that were more like caves than actual rooms. There were much nicer parts, too, all wainscoting and velvety wallpaper, giving the feel of turn-of-the-century drawing rooms.

The room I found myself in was neither of these. It was small, square, and windowless with a bare concrete floor and crudely whitewashed walls dimmed from years of disuse. I squinted hard to make more sense of my surroundings, and that's when I saw the faded blood spatter, faint rust-colored speckles that clung to the paint as though even the walls themselves craved blood.

In the corner was a table, on top of which sat an old-fashioned leather doctor's case.

I shivered. I wasn't born yesterday; I happened to know old-fashioned doctors' cases didn't bode well.

Then I spotted the bucket. It was wide and low, like something you'd find in a barn. It was full of water and—oh shit—forget doctor bags, *that* was the part of this whole thing that really freaked me out.

I heard voices. Male laughter. I imagined their pleasant chitchat.

Hi, how are you?

Brilliant, just brilliant. In the mood for a spot of torture?

The voices faded and the brisk clack of footsteps tore me from my morbid imaginings. The footsteps got closer. It was one person alone. They'd paused outside my door.

"Crap crap crap," I whispered, frantically looking around. I jerked my body back and forth, trying to free myself. But I was trapped.

Someone was coming inside.

I knew who liked torture. Who had an obsession with me.

Alcántara. On my first mission, I'd listened as he'd spent the night torturing some kid to death.

I blinked my eyes shut hard. Into my head dumped every esoteric perversion a medieval genius like Hugo de Rosas Alcántara might enjoy. Things like books bound in skin. Probing for the four humors of the human body. Strange alchemies and elixirs.

I held my breath as the door creaked open.

Not Alcántara. Headmaster Fournier.

A chuff of breath escaped me—a moment's relief—then an even more profound dread swamped me.

At least Alcántara was a known quantity. I could talk to him, distract him. But Claude Fournier was basically a stranger to me. He was genteel and ancient, and by the indifferent, impatient glint in his eye, I could tell he had no qualms whatsoever about wiping me off the face of this earth.

"Well, well." He came and stood over me, and the way he scanned me made me feel like a body on the autopsy table: already dead. "Somebody hasn't appreciated my hospitality."

Hospitality? As if.

"And me, looking out for your well-being as I have." He nodded to a spot below my feet, and I craned my head, spotting a dark puddle. A foot canted out at an unnatural angle. "Take this Trainee, for example. Rob, I think it was. I caught him attempting an indiscretion. I'll not have such discourtesy." His eyes met mine again, hard and cold. "From any of you."

Somewhere in that announcement, he was accusing me of something. I thought about denying whatever it was he was charging, but I knew better than to contradict an ancient. Instead, I lay there silently. Maybe if he said his piece, he'd feel better.

"And you have perhaps been the most ungracious of all." Fournier walked a circle around me as he spoke. "You spurn the home we've given you. And worse, you think to avail yourself of our extensive training, only to turn and use it against us? We who've fed you, clothed you?"

Nope, he wasn't looking like he felt any better.

Total panic made me all sputtery and awkward. "I...I wasn't spurning. I didn't mean to spurn, like, at all. I was just... I needed to..."

"To find your mother?" He laughed at what must've been the expression of shocked dismay on my face. He knew I had a mother. Would he seek her out to kill her himself? "You silly child. Do you think I am merely some simpering school headmaster? I am more than you'll ever understand. My reach extends further than your tiny mind could ever comprehend. I know your mother. And naturally Charlotte informed me of your plans. She was quite distressed that you took it upon yourself to murder our Alrik."

Charlotte. So she was in with the Directorate? One more slot to be filled in on my mental map of who was allied with whom.

"Do you really believe that you"—his eyes dragged along my body with disgust—"are more valuable than one such as Alrik Dagursson? Your conceit astounds me. I knew you to be arrogant. I knew you were foolish. But I had no idea of the depth of your crude, simpleminded, impulsive ways. I'd enjoy killing you even if you hadn't just tried to flee the island."

"Are you—" I was jittery, my breath coming in shallow sips. "Are you going to kill me, then?"

God help me, but I was almost relieved at the prospect. Maybe he'd at least make it quick. No buckets or bags of medieval torture devices.

"Not at first," he said. "At first, I will make you talk."

CHAPTER EIGHT

"Um. Talk?" Please please please let it not be that bad. I was good under pressure—I could sprinkle enough truths among the lies I'd tell, making my fabrications sound real. I'd protect my friends, of course. Except for Josh—he was getting thrown under the bus. But Fournier still hadn't asked anything, so I decided to get this show on the road. "What would you like to talk about?" I laughed nervously, and goddammit, why did I have to do stuff like that?

Fournier's answering smile surprised me—and not in a good way. "We are going to talk about your fears, Acari Drew." He began to stroke my hair from my face, as gently as a lover.

I was good under pressure, but this was proving to be a lot of pressure right out of the gate. My voice wavered as I said, "Fears?"

"Yes, child. Tell me, what are you afraid of?"

Losing those I loved.

But I didn't say that. It came too close to the vulnerable heart of me. To the heart of my everything.

I held his gaze, ready to flatter, making myself believe the words I spoke next. "At the moment, what I'm afraid of most is you." A white lie, but bearing truth enough.

Would he perceive the falsehood and kill me for it? Part of me hoped so. Just now, it was clear there were worse things than dying.

But he laughed. *Laughed.*

Fournier chuckled warmly and stroked my hair. His hand slid down to cup my cheek. "I know you jest, young one."

I froze. "I do?"

He tugged at the leather strap cutting across my chest. "I know that you fear being trapped here." His hand traced up my body until he was threading his fingers back through my hair, cradling my skull. His eyes dilated, and like a blot of ink spreading, they turned from blue to black. Warmth suffused my brain, but not a pleasant warmth. It was the heat of a limb held too close to a flame, or the unnatural scald of one's own blood flowing outside the body. "You fear being alone. This is why you pander like a dog to Carden."

The warmth turned cool. Then cold. Icy fingers probed my brain.

He grew still. "Ah," he said in the barest whisper. "But you are not bonded."

I hardened my features, not letting anything show.

Pulling his hand away, he sucked in a breath, assessing this new knowledge. "I see there is something I've misunderstood. Something I've missed. Perhaps I am being too subtle," he said. "Perhaps I should begin at the beginning. Addressing fears of a more physical nature."

He moved out of my line of sight and began rustling around.

I craned my neck to see what he might be doing. "Ph-physical?"

"Yes, for example"—in an abrupt movement, he grabbed

the lip of the bucket and, with very un-Fournierlike brutish-ness, he dragged it toward me with an ear-splitting scrape—"I know you fear water."

He dipped a pitcher in the bucket and splashed my face. "You fear drowning," he said, sounding almost bored. "Chok-ing." He angled his elbow, pouring the water in a heavier stream. "Sinking. The feel of water in your eyes, your ears."

I tried to be brave, really I did. I tried to hold still, to show him I wouldn't be cowed. I tried, but the water kept coming, until my most primal instincts took over, and my heels tried to hammer the table. It was no good; I was bound too securely. There was no budging. No escaping.

Ronan had taught me to swim, but only I could cure my fear. Overcoming my panic at the rush of water in my nose and mouth was something even he couldn't teach.

He pulled my head up. "Brave girl. Would you like me to stop? Shall you tell me how you convinced Tom to ferry you off the island?"

"Tom had nothing—"

The water came again, an icy deluge slapping my face.

I couldn't be brave any more. Something in me cracked, and I managed to turn away and suck in a quick breath.

He stopped pouring for a moment, and I thought I'd explode from the sheer joy of sucking air into my lungs. I coughed. Caught my breath.

"Is it someone other than the Draug Keeper?"

"Nobody is helping—"

"And still you lie." He dipped the pitcher again then grabbed my jaw and wrenched up my chin. "I know you've practiced holding your breath. How long can you hold it whilst enduring the sensation of water flowing into your nostrils?" He poured and poured without stopping, until I began to sputter and choke, but his hand held me tightly. "You fear drowning.

And it is in such visceral fears, such physical terrors, that we uncover one's more, shall we say, metaphysical secrets. Tell me, Annelise, are you ready to share your secrets?"

Finally, he shoved my chin away, wrenching my neck sideways.

I coughed until my chest ached, and then I vomited until my throat burned, spewing water, and, finally, foam. Ropes of spittle hung from my lips.

It'd been a fatal mistake to think I could outwit him. I was barely following his words—I was too busy staying alive. My mind raced. I needed to come up with something because there was no way I was giving up someone as innocent as Tom the Draug Keeper.

"Would you like me to stop? Have you aught to say? You say nobody has helped you, but surely there is one who is your ally."

He scrutinized me as my brutal hacking slowly dissipated into dry-heaves. When I finally finished, I blinked the tears from my eyes and met his gaze. I donned vampire-worthy good manners like armor. "In this, I have acted alone, Master Fournier. The arrogance and disrespect are solely my own. But I am ready to repent. I will tell you whatever you like."

Fake it till you make it, and in that instant of fakery, I felt a fresh burst of courage. Of rebellion. I didn't have much, but I did have my dignity. I refused to be broken. And I was going to buy myself some time.

He made a little *hmph* sound, then after a pause, pulled a pristine handkerchief from his breast pocket, acting the refined Fournier once more, and dabbed at my lips. "Then enough of this vulgarity. Let us be honest with each other. What role does Tracer Ronan play in your drama?"

It wasn't the question I'd expected. My breath hitched, setting off a fresh round of coughing.

I'd thought he'd ask about my escape, what I knew of my mother, and then there was Carden's mysterious cause that I kept getting hints of…but Ronan? That was one place I dared not let my mind wander. Carden was a vampire who had no trouble watching his own back. But not Ronan. I needed to keep him out of this, no matter what. I could do that one thing for him. Aside from my mother, he was the one person in this whole mess I wanted protected above all others.

Fournier had my chin between his fingers again, holding me like a vise, staring deep into my eyes. His pupils expanded, contracted, as he searched for something.

Cold fingers wended through my brain and—*holy shit*—he was in my head, probing.

Ronan had the power of persuasion, and he'd once told me how I was one of the few people who was strong enough to fight it. And so that's what I did. I gritted my teeth and fought. I didn't know what I was doing, but I put up barriers, pushing away the cold, concentrating on my pulse, my breath, anything that'd keep Fournier away.

"Fascinating." Disturbingly, he grinned. "You're clever. But I'm more than you're used to." He let go of me and clapped his hands together like he needed to brush off dirt. "Though you do surprise me, on many levels. Your strengths. Your… passions."

The slightest twitch in his brow told me he maybe even respected that. I made myself give him a nod, as if his esteem mattered.

He leaned in close and pinned his eyes on me, holding me in place as surely as his hand had. "Most girls are vulnerable to those of the Vampire persuasion. But you have never been most girls, have you, Acari Drew? Perhaps it isn't physical fear that's your undoing. Perhaps it is a Tracer who is your weakness."

A Tracer. *Ronan.*

I hadn't fooled him for a second. And as Fournier spoke the words, more than ever, I felt the depth and the truth of my feelings for Ronan.

And with it came a knowledge that was bright and clear and true: Fournier could drown me all day, but I'd never let him see how much Ronan meant to me.

"Tracer Ronan means nothing—"

He smacked me. Hard.

"Don't be coy. You'll answer my questions, or I'll explore the topic of your fears in greater depth."

There wasn't anything in this room he could subject me to that'd be worse than losing someone else I loved. I considered the doctor's bag and something inside me died. But the answer would just have to be *bring it on.*

Fatalism made my voice firm. "Tracer Ronan is my teacher. That's it. He's all right, I guess."

Fournier studied me, his lips pursed like he was being forced to smell something really gross. He didn't seem to be buying it, but he wasn't not buying it, either. Maybe I was stronger than he realized.

"That is your answer?" he said after a moment. "Tracer Ronan is your teacher and nothing more? You believe he is faithful to Vampire above all others?"

I managed a nod, the terror clutching my throat, making it hard to speak.

Fournier's eyes narrowed. "More loyal to us than he is to you?"

"Yes," I rasped. "Of course."

"Hmm..." He considered me, and just when I thought maybe I'd convinced him, a smile curled one corner of his mouth. I was only now getting acquainted with Headmaster

Fournier, but I knew what that smile meant. "I'm told to beware of ladies who protest too much."

He strolled to the table in the corner, wiping his hands on a cloth. "But no matter. There are those who plot against us, and I shall get at the truth. I suppose I'll just need to probe more deeply. Or rather...not I. There are others to probe for me. I tire of your charade. But Hugo is tireless. Yes," he added with a smile. He'd caught the panic in my eyes. "I speak of Master Alcántara. As you know, he has more of an appetite for torture than I."

He reached for the door. Opened it. Stepped back.

I craned my head back, tracking his line of sight.

Alcántara.

Fournier tipped his head toward the Spanish vampire as he left the room. "Enjoy."

CHAPTER NINE

As Alcántara's attention melted into me, he touched his hand to his heart with a small bow. "What a pleasure to have you here, spread before me, a feast for one starved." He must've seen something in my expression that amused him because a slow grin spread across his face. "That is right. You are mine now, *querida*. What think you of that?"

I didn't think much of it, obviously. This guy gave me the serious, old-fashioned creeps. And by the hungry look in his eye, I feared I was in real trouble now. *Out of the frying pan* and all that.

But I clenched back the shudder that was threatening to spring from the base of my spine. "I think I'm glad the headmaster is gone."

He chuckled. "Indeed." He traced a languorous finger down my cheek, pausing beneath my chin. "And are you happy I am here?"

Oh crap.

I needed to stall. To buy some time. "Are you working with

Fournier?" Instantly, I bit my lip, fearing the words came out too much like a challenge.

But Alcántara shocked me when, instead of getting upset, he simply expelled an impatient breath. "Must we speak of him? So consumed by political matters, he is. It is entirely lacking in couth. Fournier desires the quick victory, but mine is a deeper sort of game. While he is thinking of politics, I pursue a different kind of power."

That didn't bode well for me, bound as I was to a table. I gulped hard. "So, uh, not a politician?"

"Not I, no. Politicking is for the simpleminded. Fournier builds an army of pawns, whereas I see the entire chessboard. And so I am patient, allowing the game to unfold. Rather than short-term grasping, I content myself with books, studies." He drew his thumb along my lip and down to pinch my chin. "Other such amusements."

Oh hell no. I couldn't help but notice I was pretty much the only "amusement" in the room—unless you went for old bags and empty buckets, and somehow I didn't think that was Alcántara's thing.

I gave a nervous laugh. "Well, you know, I'm with you on the book thing. Love the old books. And you have quite the collection. In particular, I loved when you showed me—"

He pinched harder. "I'm told you were going to leave without saying goodbye."

"A *total* misunderstanding. Those Trainees came for me, and sure, I shouldn't have been out past curfew, but I like to challenge myself with the occasional brisk night swim. You remember how swimming used to freak me out? Well, I've been practicing, but I should've told someone what I was doing. In my defense, it seems I've been punished accordingly." I wriggled my shoulders and gave him my most innocent smile. "So maybe you can let me free?"

As I was babbling, all I could think about was the misericordia in my boot. Could he smell it? Sense it somehow? It had belonged to Sonja, the high priestess of this whole place. Alcántara reported to her. It'd probably mean major brownie points if he were to return it to her.

"A swim?" He eyed me. "In these clothes? I wonder…" He grabbed a handful of fabric at my belly, feeling all the layers I'd donned. "It seems you'd sink, no?"

"I like a challenge?" It was a last-ditch effort delivered with childlike uncertainty.

Bizarrely, Alcántara began to laugh. "Always you amuse, little one." And even more bizarrely, he began to unbuckle my leather bands.

"What's happening now?" I ask uneasily.

"You are young yet, and so I'd see you live." He paused to let those coal-black eyes lock with mine. "Soon a new power will rise, and when it does, you will remember this day. You will remember your friends and what they have done for you."

Did he just call me his friend? Was he letting me go? I wouldn't believe I was free until the fresh air was in my lungs. Slowly I sat up, rubbing my chest where the bands had cut into me. "For sure. And…thanks."

"All I ask is that, when your moment comes, you will remember what is important."

"Friends. What they've done for me." Check and check. They were the replies I thought he wanted to hear. Now if he'd just let me out of this room. All this weirdness had sent my heart pounding.

His eyes hardened. "Heed me, Annelise. This is not to be taken lightly. You are one to whom much has been given. You must value your intellect. Your ancestry. As those in power neglect their ideals in pursuit of blind dominion and brute control, they forget what we value most. They forget how the source of true power springs from the purity of blood. Purity of intent."

Sounded a little Hitler-y to me, but who was I to argue? I was free. "Uh, yeah, for sure." Alcántara could yammer all day about what was important to him, but I didn't forget what I valued, and that was saving my mother. I scooted to the edge of the table. Mentally, I was so out of there. "And, Master Alcántara, I am sorry."

His expression became blank and cold. "No more lies. No more attitude. You will be authentic with me. Or I will wash my hands of you."

I froze, and my face must've looked as wild as my thoughts, because he softened again. "Such doubt you have. Do you not yet trust me? I thought we'd reached an understanding."

"Of course." Though my reply came quickly, I found myself adjusting to sit cross-legged—all the closer to my weaponry. "So, just to make sure I'm following...you're saying you're getting me out of here alive?"

He grinned, and it was a creepy, creepy sight. "No, *querida*." He took my hand and guided me off the table. "I'm getting you out of here dead."

Every part of me shot to high alert. The misericordia was burning a hole in my boot, but with one hand in Alcántara's, I wouldn't be able to reach it quickly enough. "Uh...dead? I'm not really ready for dead."

Why wasn't he making any moves? I needed *him* to be the one to attack first. He'd see me coming a mile away—when it came to speed, I'd never beat him.

And then it hit me...*oh, crap*...he was going to make me a vampire.

I studied his face, trying to decipher his intent, but he'd used his free hand to slide a device from his pocket—I'd once seen Watcher Priti with the same thing—and was focused on his thumb as it danced over the surface.

Was Alcántara *texting* someone?

"So, about this get-me-out-dead thing..." I tried to tug my hand free, but he wouldn't let me go.

Instead, he squeezed my fingers, his eyes meeting mine. "I sense your fear as it thrums with every beat of your heart. But there is no need to be afraid." He slid his hand from mine and knelt beside the Trainee sprawled dead on the floor. "Shall I explain?"

A small curved blade appeared in his fingers, and when he spoke again, it was over the crackle of fabric as he sawed down the center of Rob's sweater. "Nature has many lessons to teach us. For example, some animals feign death to avoid predators."

Feigning death? Some of the tension between my shoulders relaxed. "So...you don't want me dead-dead?"

"*Por supuesto que no, cariño.* You will merely feign death to escape the keep." With a flick of his wrist, he sliced the Trainee's carotid artery on the side of his neck. "But we must make it realistic. We must camouflage you. And there is nothing more repellant to a vampire than the scent of half-turned blood."

"How are you going to—?" And then I smelled it—I smelled the blood before I saw it—a blast hitting me like the stench of rotten things left too long under a hot sun. "Oh." Thicker and darker than normal human blood, it flowed sluggishly, forming a shining black moon on the floor. "Ew."

He began to make other, deeper cuts along the Trainee's body.

I couldn't suppress a shudder. "Isn't that enough?"

"You hope it will be. My plan is audacious, but it is not foolproof. It requires much gore. Under which you will need to lie utterly still."

I glanced from Alcántara to the body and back again. "You want me to be *in* all that?"

At his nod, my stomach pulsed and spit filled my mouth with the urge to retch. I buried my nose in the crook of my elbow. "Can't."

"You can, *querida*." He rose, and it was amazing how, after all that, his clothes were completely spotless. "And you will. I risk much to help you. Even now the gravedigger comes for you. We shall wrap you up and he will cart you away from here like so much carnage."

A rap on the door a moment later brought a tall figure in a long black cloak, his face hidden under a deep hood.

I took a step back, feeling all kinds of trepidation. Why should I suddenly start to trust Alcántara? "Gravedigger or grim reaper?"

His body was crooked, leaning over an old wheelbarrow. Silently, he pulled aside a musty swath of burlap.

I peered at the dinged metal. "Is that rust or old blood?" My question was met by silence, and I looked up, trying to discern the gravedigger's face. "You want me to climb into that?"

But even as I said it, I knew. Either I seized this maybe-shot at freedom, or it'd be Fournier and his army of Trainee pinheads for me.

Alcántara glared impatiently. "We do not have much time."

"I'm in, I'm in." I clambered into the wheelbarrow and curled into a ball.

They draped the burlap over me, and the fabric was heavy with the smell of cheese and sweat and decay. I covered my face with my hands, curling tighter, pinching off the sneezing fit I was desperate to let loose.

And then the wetness came. The blood, still warm from the Trainee's body, was heavy, feeling less like liquid and more like melted tar being splashed onto me with dull, wet slaps.

When the first body part was tossed atop me, I had to recede deep into my mind. I tried to imagine myself any place but here. But more and more toppled onto me, until I felt like I might drown in the carnage.

I tried concentrating on the image of my mother. I was doing this for her. I would see her. Know her. Save her.

The weight of the gore became unbearable. Each breath in and out was a battle—the sensation was of inhaling blood, not oxygen. I was choking on it.

My mind couldn't hold onto the image of my mother. Thoughts of her mingled with the blood, and I made myself imagine this my rebirth.

The old me was dying. The old Drew, who'd once chosen this island, would disappear from the face of it. I would die this fake death only to emerge from the carnage as a new person.

I would be reborn.

Voices entered my consciousness, and I held onto each word like a lifeline.

"Take the child," I heard Alcántara say to the gravedigger. "And do not lose her again."

"I'll protect her better than you ever could," a male voice said in reply.

It was Carden.

CHAPTER TEN

What. The. Hell.

Carden?

Since when was he allied with Alcántara?

These were the thoughts rumbling through my head as he wheeled me out of the keep. Generally, I tried not to dwell on things, but this was one mental loop I clung to. Anger was so much easier to process than the terror that nagged me.

Because the only thing more frightening than the ancient wheelbarrow's *squeak-squeak* as it echoed through the cavernous halls of the keep was when the squeaking stopped. When Carden would let go the cart's handles to speak, masking his accent in hushed tones, and male voices mingled with his, asking questions, giving orders.

I held my breath, grateful I had yet to hear the voice that scared me above all others—the voice of Sonja, queen of them all.

Reborn, I reminded myself. A new person. A courageous person—one who walked alone, made her own rules.

One who wasn't freaking out, buried beneath pounds and pounds of foul gore.

Carden pressed on, and just when it felt like he was going to spend the rest of eternity wheeling me in my own personal horror show, suffocating and scared, his voice came to me in a rough whisper. "Almost there."

Even from beneath the layers of burlap and carnage, I felt the temperature plunge. Carden stopped, and I held my breath, tensing and straining to detect where we were and who else might be around.

But we were alone, and he began to heave chunks of Trainee off of me.

A blessed blast of air hit my skin, and I shivered with pleasure as he peeled away the heavy layers of fabric. It'd stuck to my skin and made a horrific wet sucking sound as it separated from my body.

I blinked to clear my eyes, but it didn't get any brighter. I propped myself up on an elbow, trying in the near-darkness to make sense of where he'd brought me. A single torch hissed and popped as it cast slashes of gold and black dancing along rough-hewn rock walls. Wherever the light caught, gleamed with dampness. I tuned into the distant *plip-plip* of water and the sulfurous stench of underground springs.

This was one of the caverns beneath the vampires' cliff-top keep.

"We're still here? After all that, I thought we'd be in, like, Finland by now." I was wiping the gore from my face when my hand froze.

In one swift movement, Carden pulled the hooded cloak from his body. Torchlight danced across his hardened form, glittering along the thick sword that hung at his side. He wore his kilt, but even that looked dangerous, a thick dark mass of wool gathered around his waist and sweeping over his shoulder, held in place with a crude little dagger.

This was the Carden of old. A vampire *and* a warrior. And his eyes were boring down at me, his expression unreadable.

It seemed I wasn't the only one who'd turned a new leaf.

A different sort of fear began to pulse through my blood. Was he still angry with me? How would things be between us?

Nervous, all I could think to say was, "Hi to you, too." It came out sounding more like a question than an actual greeting. "I, uh, like your sword."

Inexplicably, this made me blush, and I cursed myself under my breath.

His face softened, and he briefly shut his eyes with a shake of his head. "Och, and hi yourself, dove." He reached a hand down to help me out.

"Thanks." I gave him a relieved and grateful smile that felt like it had originated from my toes. "I mean, in a big way. Thank you for coming for me."

"As if I wouldn't." He caught me as I stumbled on my cramped legs, but then he grimaced.

I realized I must've looked—and smelled—disgusting. "I'm pretty gross, huh?"

He tapped the tip of my nose with his fingertip. "A bit unpalatable, yes. But nothing a leap into the sea won't fix."

"Great," I grumbled, looking around to see where we were. Because of course our escape couldn't be as simple as strolling out the front door.

A few tunnels extended around us like spokes from a wheel. I didn't know which scared me more, the passage that was pitch black or those that shone with torchlight.

Our location clicked. A fine needle of dread pierced me. I knew this place.

"We're near the sea gate," I said, trying to make myself

sound more confident than I currently felt. Deep beneath vampire central, I'd come this way when I'd broken into their lair what felt like a lifetime ago. I'd made my way out again, but I'd never be able to escape the memory of the horrors I'd seen that day.

I assumed we weren't going back the way we came, which meant the only way out was through that pitch-black tunnel. It led to a cliffside gate that dropped off into thin air—and that wasn't even the scariest part of this whole thing. The scariest part would be the freezing waves churning and crashing against the rocks below.

"How high is the tide?" I asked, not even sure what I wanted the answer to be.

"High enough. We must hurry." Carden waved me into the exit tunnel, needing to duck lower the closer we got to the gate. "Ready for a sea bath?"

I dragged my feet, wanting a second to wrap my mind around what we were about to do. "Do I have a choice?"

But then faint voices carried to us, echoing along the tunnel walls. I tilted my head, straining to listen, but sound played tricks here. The speakers could be ten feet away or ten times that.

"Come, lass." He snatched my hand and pulled me into a jog. We were quickly plunged into total blackness, and I must've gripped his hand too hard or made an anxious noise, because suddenly the old Carden was back with me, squeezing my hand, speaking with an easy lilt. "I've always wanted a swim with you."

For a second I thought it was just my eyes adjusting, but I soon realized the tunnel was getting lighter. How long had I been inside? It was the dimming, which meant the sky never got brighter than a dreary gunmetal gray.

"Where's the light coming from?" I squinted, trying to

make sense of it. "Is that a spotlight? Do they have search—" I slammed into Carden's back as he stopped short. "What—?"

He clapped a hand to my mouth. *"Wheesht."*

And then I heard it. Heard *her.*

Sonja, her voice vibrating above all the others, saying, "Find them."

We broke into an awkward run. I slammed my forehead against a low rock and stumbled, swooning with pain. But Carden grabbed me, and wrapping a tight arm around my chest, he began to haul me the rest of the way.

But it wasn't necessary. I was racing on my own power now. I was so out of there.

"We must—" he began, but I didn't care to hear what he had to say. The sea gate was in my sights now, and it was propped and hanging open.

I hurtled through it and flung myself over the edge.

I sucked in a breath, then instinct kicked in. I was falling, falling, but managed to right myself, tucking my elbows tight to my body, pinching my nose, aiming my toes down. To avoid smashing my bones against the hard surface of the water, it was critical to soften my muscles, and I relaxed my body—at least as much as one could while hurtling into the sea. I wouldn't say I sliced neatly into the waves, but I didn't break anything, either.

Still, I hit the surface hard enough to momentarily blacken my vision. I came to as I was kicking my way up, and was sucking in my first gulp air before my thoughts had even cleared.

Thank you, Ronan, for so many months of rigorous train-ing. I could do this unconscious...and almost had.

I didn't have a second to spend with that thought when a wave slapped me from behind. And then another. They were relentless, coming one after the other, hitting me, pushing me down. I tumbled and rolled in the black sea. I was thrown against rocks. My feet caught on them at the bottom. They cut my hands, my face. Impenetrable blades of granite all around.

I refused to die in this water.

I kicked and flailed and used everything I had to propel myself away from the craggy shoreline and swam deeper into the water, until finally I made it past the break.

The waves were softer and rounder here, but no less dangerous. These rollers had the force of giants. Massive swells bobbed me up and pitched me down, able to drown me just as surely as the choppy breakers.

Where was Carden? I scanned up the cliffside to the sea gate. A figure was peering out, scanning the horizon. A figure... lit by a spotlight.

I gasped a quick lungful of air and dove under. I knew a moment's panic—was that Carden up there?—but then a hand grabbed my arm and pulled me back up.

His voice was husky in my ear. "You've lost your mind, lass."

"You could say I'm a new woman."

"I like it. Och," he blurted and tugged me hard, out of the blaze of a roving searchlight. "Hold your breath. They hunt for us."

Before I could say anything, he pulled me under. My arms cramped and my lungs burned, but we swam and swam, and when I thought I couldn't make it any farther, Carden grabbed my upper arm hard enough to leave a bruise and dragged me the last few yards.

With a kick, he heaved me above the water's surface just as a rowboat splashed up beside us.

I tried to grab hold of the side, but the craft was tiny, pitching and rearing on the rough water. "Hurry," a voice rasped from inside.

A gloved hand grabbed me as Carden shoved at my butt, and I toppled like a dead fish into the belly of the boat.

A pair of eyes stared at me from beneath a wool fisherman's cap. "Cain't say I won't be pleased to see your backside, lass."

Did Tom the Draug Keeper just make a comment about my backside?

I glared at him. "Excuse me?"

"Stop your gawping." He spat into the water.

Carden dropped into the boat. "He only means he wants you gone."

"Yeah, well, I want me gone, too." I flinched, reacting just in time as Carden tossed something to me. It was my duffel.

"Hey, awesome. Where'd this come from?"

"I found it on the path. It's how I knew you'd been taken. You'd never abandon your wee rucksack."

He peered inside as I unzipped it and rifled the contents. Hammerfest, Norway was north of the Arctic Circle, and I'd packed accordingly, bringing every warm item of clothing I owned.

I shivered, thinking there wasn't a parka in the world that could've eased the chill that'd settled into my bones. Seeing the stuff that I'd packed what felt like a thousand years ago brought home what I was doing.

"Get some dry clothes on before you catch your death," Carden said with a grin that was too jaunty for my tastes.

"Yes, sir," I muttered, though I was grateful for the fresh change of clothing. I stopped talking after that. Getting dressed while neither exposing myself nor tumbling out of the wildly bobbing boat demanded all my attention. Finally, I dropped onto the bench, no longer freezing and only slightly damp. "Is this thing even sea-worthy?"

"My boat's a braw thing." Tom set to rowing. "You're the one's gonna get us all kill't."

"What?" I gave him an overly innocent look. "I'm sitting."

"I mean your addlepated notions of escape." The way Tom said it sounded like *excape.*

Carden laughed, low and resigned, and gave a quick half-hug around my shoulders. "What can I say? This is *your* plan, love."

CHAPTER ELEVEN

Carden joined Tom at the oars, and after several minutes of rowing—plus a fair amount of whispered curses—the search-light had shrunk to a pale disc in the far distance.

I turned on Carden the moment we were far enough away to start the engines. "We need to discuss this Alcántara thing."

"What Alcántara thing?" He reached into his bag and pulled out a small leather pouch. "A wee gift for you, to show my appreciation."

"You're avoiding the topic." I took the pouch from him. It had an intriguing heft to it. But, no. I wouldn't be distracted. "Don't try to change the subject. You know what thing. Since when are you two friends?"

"We're not friends," he said flatly, and set to stowing his oars. "Are you not going to look at my gift?"

"I may be hundreds of years younger than you, but I wasn't born yesterday. Tell me what's really going on." I stared at him, waiting for a better answer, but he only stared right back. "Okay, fine. Wee giftie."

But then I felt like an ungrateful shrew, because in that

pouch was the most amazing weapon I'd ever seen. It was a throwing star, but one like I'd never seen before. Two-pointed, in the shape of an S. A very sharp, very lethal S. "Ohmygod, Carden. It's…it's amazing. I've never seen such a thing."

He seemed pleased. "I thought you might take a fancy to it."

"I do. Thank you." I *was* so very grateful. But also very aware that the conversation had gotten off the topic of Alcántara.

Tom piped up, "War finds men peculiar bedfellows."

My cheeks blazed. "Excuse me?"

The old Draug Keeper sucked on his teeth. "You asked 'boot the Spaniard"—pronounced *Spainyerd*—"he's who all I'm talking about. When fighting starts, in your bed you might find one you thought was your enemy."

"Not the way I'd have put it." Carden rubbed his face with a sigh. "But, aye. Alcántara wants Fournier ousted just as much as I." He closed my hand gently over my new weapon and leaned close to whisper, "I'm glad you like it. When you throw it, it will come back to you. Like a wee boomerang. Lethal grace. Like you, dove. And, like the star, I hope you always return to me."

Some unknown feeling filled me. Was it love? Trepidation? Regardless, it was more emotion than was safe.

I cleared my throat and returned to the topic. They both seemed in a talkative mood, and I knew better than to miss my chance at answers. "So is Alcántara also allied with Freya?" I still couldn't figure how Sonja's sister fit into all this.

"Alcántara is allies with Alcántara." Carden nestled closer to me on the floor of the boat. "And that is that."

I turned to him, ready to proceed with my interrogation, but couldn't help laughing instead. Carden's hair was wet and scraggly from the endless splash of waves over the sides. His kilt and cloak were soaked, and the stink of the boat—something like petrol, goat poop, and marine slime—clung to the wool.

"Who's the aromatic one now?" I bit my cheek to lessen my grin. "Though you did tell Ronan you wanted, what was it, the sea breeze on your cheeks?"

"Careful or I'll punish you." He glared, but I knew him well enough now to tell he was only playing. He must've seen the impertinence in my eyes, because his narrowed. "You doubt me, do you?"

"You don't scare me." I nudged him with an elbow. "You're all talk."

I squealed as he grabbed me and pulled me onto him.

"Ah, you make a fine wee lap blanket." He nestled me into place, and I curled into him with a sigh, overcome by the sensation of safety and comfort I always knew in Carden's presence.

I began to relax. I was free—the island was at my back. We were on our way. For now, there was nothing to do but sit in the boat and enjoy my vampire's company.

I tilted my chin to give him a quick kiss. It seemed that, with or without the bond, I really did love the guy.

"So we've a boat to a floatplane to another boat?" He adjusted beneath me with a curse. Now that I was on his lap, it was *his* butt that'd be suffering the full brunt of sloshing sea water. "Is this a journey or a test of my affections?"

His words had been playful, but I couldn't let go of the memory of Alcántara's last words. *Do not lose her again.* "Affection has nothing to do with it." I shrugged, my throat gone tight. "It seems to me like you were forced to come."

"Och, silly lass. Affection has everything to do with it." He settled me deeper into his lap. "That Spanish bastard hasn't the power to force aught from me." He planted a quick kiss on my forehead. "Nae, it's simply that I don't want that lovesick pup, Ronan, to get all the glory."

I laughed, even though my heart twisted to hear his name. *Ronan.* When we'd said our goodbye, I'd been frantic to be on my way. He'd seemed sad, but how could he be when he'd discovered his sister lived? I pushed aside the knowledge of what she'd done to my friends. Family was the most important thing to him, right? More important than me, surely.

Regardless, he wasn't my *pup* any longer. Honestly, I doubted he'd ever been.

"Did you see him before you left?" I asked.

"Ronan? No. Freya wants him back where he belongs. I'd say the boy has more to occupy him than he can handle."

The tightness in my throat became a burn.

Focus. I needed to focus on the task at hand. The island—and Ronan—were behind me now.

I was off to traffic in death. It'd be naive of me to think otherwise. Someone would be killed—me, my mother, or Charlotte. I had to do everything in my power to make sure the only one to suffer was option number three.

Sorry, Ronan.

My throat was burning. Time for a topic change.

I leaned back to catch Carden's eye. "So what kind of name is Hammerfest, anyway? Sounds like some sort of heavy metal thing."

He grunted. "Norway. Makes sense. The old ones do like the dark."

Familiar dread curled through me. It was polar night in that part of the world, which meant over a couple of months of no sunlight. As in, no light...*at all*. Complete darkness.

The undead would be out in droves.

I triple-checked my weapons, flexing wrists and calves, seeking their reassuring pressure. The misericordia I carried in secret seemed to pulse in my boot, making me raw with energy. "Yeah. Polar night. Sounds freaky."

"Sounds *heavenly*." Carden stretched till his limbs popped. "No sun for over two months."

"It won't matter anyway. The island we're going to is one giant factory. We'll be inside, I guess."

"You guess? That's your plan for us?" He laughed low. "You guess we'll wander in and have a look about?"

"We have to deal with the tunnel first," I mumbled. The island was the endpoint of an undersea pipeline; it was connected to the mainland by Melkøysund Tunnel...a presumably heavily guarded Melkøysund Tunnel. I'd been putting off addressing that bit with Carden.

"Annelise—"

I heard the warning in his tone and quickly cut him off. "It's my mother we're talking about. I have to find her."

"It's not the tunnel that concerns me. The guards will be a lark. I'll relish taking down any Synod creature who dares cross our path. It is secrets that concern me." I felt him grow serious. "I must know. You met Charlotte and waited to tell me. Is this why you wanted the bond broken? There are things you wish to hide?"

Gulp. And how. But I pushed those very things from my mind. That life was behind me now. Ronan was behind me.

I had to take a steadying breath before replying, "It has nothing to do with the bond. I told you why I wanted to sever it. I didn't tell you about Charlotte because I didn't want you to worry." That was close enough to the truth. To *a* truth. For good measure, I added, "Charlotte's not a big fan of mine."

He surprised me with a quick laugh. "She wouldn't be. She's not a fan of much." He grew thoughtful. "I believe she's helping Sonja and the Directorate make an alliance with Jacob."

"What? Why?" I thought about Ronan, and what I knew of his powerful lineage. That same Celtic blood ran through Charlotte's veins. "Wouldn't she be, like, a queen in Freya's world? A queen among queens."

"She never liked competition, our Lottie. I don't think she'd fancy having other queens about." His expression grew grim. "It remains to be seen how she'll take to Sonja's rule." His head dropped back against the hull. "So, we're on a boat, off to kill Ronan's sister."

"We might not need to kill her," I said quickly.

He only raised his brows at that.

"We're going to save my mom." I gave his chest a little punch. "Positive thoughts, Carden."

"As you say." He snuggled me closer, deep in thought.

We sat in silence for some time. Just as I was drifting off, his low rasp cut through my sleepy thoughts. "I feel it, you know. How you're torn in his presence."

I stiffened, suddenly wide awake. "What are you talking about?" I'd managed to sound off-handed, even as my stomach was doing flip-flops.

"Not what. Who." He tipped his chin to catch my eye. "You know I speak of Ronan. Even without the bond, I feel it. I feel your doubts. I know your feelings. I know you care for the boy. Your heart holds no secrets from me. But bond or no, we belong together." He gripped me tightly, almost too tightly. "You're mine."

He growled that last bit, and it sent all my girl parts aflutter.

I gazed up at him. I did care for Ronan. But accidental kisses and a turbulent crush didn't make a relationship real.

Carden, though, was here. Now. With me.

That was real.

"Of course I care for Ronan," I said. "He's my friend."

There was a pause, and then a smile slid onto Carden's face. "As long as that's all he is," he said with a pinch to my bottom.

I didn't want to think about how I'd maybe just lied, just the tiniest bit.

I decided it was a great time for me to turn the spotlight around to Carden. "Speaking of Ronan, what did he mean when he said how much you love your cause?"

I'd always wondered what kept my vampire on the island. We'd been bonded, yes, but it had to be more than that, especially now that I knew how relatively easily that bond could be altered.

He was silent, so I pressed, "Why do you put up with Alcántara? You clearly don't like the guy. You don't really like any of them. So why not just leave for good?"

He'd always managed to evade my questions about his past, and I expected the same now. And so he shocked me when he said, "It was vampires who saved me long ago."

I sat up at this. "Wait, I thought it was vampires who'd killed you."

He tsked and shook his head. "You know Culloden, aye?"

"A battle in Scotland, right?"

"The *last* battle in Scotland. It took less than an hour for a couple thousand men, the clan system, and the heart of Gaelic culture to be demolished. But a wee healer roamed the moor after battle. She found the men who survived and promised them revenge."

My mind spun with possibilities. "This healer was...Sonja?"

"Och, no," he spat. "Sonja had already taken over *Eyja næturinnar* by then, done her own bit of ruination. The one who came to me was her sister. Freya. She was building an army. She offered to turn me. I welcomed it."

I deflated beneath the sudden weight of it all. So much

slaughter and conflict—it all seemed so pointless. "Great. You went from fighting in one army to fighting for another."

"You listen," Carden snapped, "but you don't hear." The scold in his voice took me aback. "Freya turned me, yes, but then she released me. I was able to return to my home. To my mother and sisters, who were alone. I was the last man, see. The last of my family. But Freya let me go to them, to protect them."

My eyes widened. "You have vampire sisters?"

A sharp crack of a laugh escaped him. "Bloody hell, no. That would've...my sisters..." He was lost a moment in memories, a faint mingling of humor and sadness playing across his features. "They'd have torn me limb-from-limb." He gave a sharp sniff, seeming to snap back into the conversation. "No, my mother and sisters died as old women. All of them. As it should've been."

He turned his gaze back on me. "And so I owed Freya a debt. She gave me the gift of my family's safety. I watched nieces and nephews born, then grandnieces and grand-nephews. I watched a generation grow old and die until the day came when I had to leave." A sad smile crooked his cheek. "Such a young uncle was too suspicious, see. And so I returned to Freya." With a finger on my cheek, he guided my eyes back to his. "I see your suspicion, and I assure you, lass, it's not just my honor that has me siding with Freya. I believe in her cause —it's *my* cause, as well. To this day, I am hers to use as she will."

The bolt of jealousy was sudden. I peered at him. "To use... how?"

He chucked my chin. "Not like that, love. I'm useful, well, for the cause Ronan was talking about. We've vowed to restore Vampiracy to the old ways. To restore the pure Celtic lines. How it was before people like Dagursson and Fournier and

Jacob came sniffing around, seeking wealth and domination. They want to rule the world—"

I stopped him with a hand to his arm. "Wait. Like, the *world* world? As in away from the Isle of Night?"

Carden sneered. "Naturally. The fools. They amassed their armies with no respect for the bloodlines. Why do you think so many Trainees and Acari die? They were not born to this. But such like Fournier have an infinite desire for more beneath them, serving them. They aren't choosy. They demand more children for more vampires, for more power, and so the blood has gotten diluted." He sat tall, and with a clap to his chest, declared, "We are creatures of power and beauty, not little Napoleons. But these men have corrupted what it means to be Vampire. Fournier, Jacob and his Synod, they are petty tyrants who don't understand our old ways. We were creatures of the land. We were truly powerful, living in balance, the men *and* the women. We were magnificent predators. Pure of heart."

"Alcántara mentioned something about purity," I said, then paused. "But wait—he's Spanish, not Celtic at all."

"True enough. He believes the bloodlines are even older than that. All those books of his," Carden said dismissively. "Some humans question the meaning of life. Well, some vampires are no different. In his books, his mathematics, Alcántara is seeking the meaning of it all. He believes there's one pure and essential truth to be found."

I wanted to ask if it was honestly possible for a blood-thirsty predator to be pure of heart, but I thought better of interrupting this speech. All this time, Carden had been protecting me from vampire politics, and now I was hanging on every word.

"You ask what my cause is," he went on. "I'm a man of honor, and men of honor pay their debts. I owe Freya, but for me it goes still deeper than that. It's the principle of the thing, aye? It's time to right the wrongs and put things back into their proper order. It's time to overthrow those who've installed themselves by brute force—those who turn children not ready for our world into counterfeit warriors so that they might climb up a ladder of bodies in their quest for more and more power. They are whom I fight. And I report to Freya, as a soldier would to his general. It is to her I've sworn my fealty. And I'm a man of my word. I would sacrifice it all for Freya to use as she will."

"So you'd sacrifice...anything?"

"Aye," he said with a firm nod. "Anything."

I thought back to the ceremony I witnessed in the vampires' keep. The chilling discovery of Sonja using the bodies of girls to strengthen her own army. And memories of a conversation overheard between Alcántara and Sonja. Sonja had wanted me. My blood. But the Spanish vampire had—inexplicably—protected me.

Did I have a powerful lineage like Carden or Ronan? Maybe even more powerful? Is that why my mother was being held prisoner?

"What if Freya said she needed *me*?" I asked quietly. "Wanted me dead?"

He planted a hard kiss on my forehead. "Foolish question from a foolish girl. Freya doesn't want you dead."

I pulled back, unable to shake the feeling that there was a bounty on my head or something. "Do you mean she wants me to live, or she wants me alive? Because there's a difference."

Did Freya want to absorb me into her vampire army? Did *Carden* want that? Because, though he loved me, it sure didn't sound like he had plans to leave her any time soon.

He peered down at me as though trying to read into my soul. "Stop your fretting. It's Charlotte and the Synod I'm worried about. And I'd give my own life before seeing them take you."

He kissed me then. Hard.

He thoroughly kissed the concerns from my mind.

Or at least he tried.

Because a seed had been planted.

CHAPTER TWELVE

We'd taken a boat to a floatplane to a cargo ship before we finally arrived at our destination: Hammerfest, Norway, one of the northernmost cities in the world. It was still early evening, but polar night had begun, which meant the sky was the color of a bruise and getting darker by the minute. The sun had set and it wouldn't be popping back up over the horizon for a good, oh, fifteen hundred hours.

"This is for us?" I asked, looking at the ancient motorcycle parked off the docks. "You sure?"

Carden nodded but didn't elaborate. I didn't know who'd left it, but presumably it was the same people who tended the safe house we were headed to. The plan was to head to a secure place to get our bearings, I'd get some rest, then we'd find our way to the island of Melkøya—hopefully using something other than a freaking boat to take us. The ground still felt as though it swayed under my feet.

He lashed our duffels to the back of the motorcycle, slid his sword neatly along the side, and patted the seat. "Up you get."

I didn't question. I was just thrilled to be traveling on something that didn't require a life jacket.

From the docks, we drove through a blink-and-you'll-miss-it fishing village lined with nondescript buildings that looked like they were built from a giant monochromatic Lego set. If it hadn't been for the occasional other driver, I'd have thought it was a ghost town. I snuck a quick look at my watch, thinking I'd somehow lost track of time, but no, it was just after five o'clock and there were hardly any people to be seen.

He reached back, grabbed my hand, and brought my arm back around his waist. "Hold on."

Already we were leaving the center of Hammerfest behind, and Carden accelerated as the road emptied and began to twist and turn. Here on the outskirts, it felt a little like the Isle of Night, with the churning sea on one edge and a wall of rock on the other. Patches of snow glowed eerily on the side of the road, flickering past us, caught in the motorcycle's high beam.

"It's actually kind of pretty," I shouted to him.

He shouted back to me, "Be happy. The last summit was held in Norilsk."

"Siberia?" I asked, and at his nod, I added, "That would've sucked. I've had only a few semesters of Norwegian, and it's already ten million times stronger than my Russian."

"Doesn't matter..." He said something else, but it got lost in the wind.

"What?"

"I said they'll mostly speak English at the summit, maybe some German."

Conversation was too hard, so I just nodded and wrapped my arms more tightly around his waist, nestling close to his back.

The engine hummed and the seat vibrated beneath me. I felt alive, excitement thrumming through me. Carden didn't speak, but he must've felt the same way, because he revved and leaned down, opening up that old bike as fast as it could go.

I inhaled deeply, filling my lungs with sea air. Frigid wind whipped me, but I didn't care. I was free. Or almost.

My mother was close. I'd find her, save her. I'd begin a new life.

We...we would begin a new life. Though, as exciting as it was, I found it difficult to picture. Where would my mother and I go? Would Carden want to come? It was hard to imagine. It felt as though I'd been on the Isle of Night forever, studying, surviving.

With Ronan.

I turned my cheek into the wind, letting the cold wind slap my cheeks and clear my mind.

A new set of smells hit me. The briny air began to mingle with some other scent, an industrial smell, like burning chemicals. And, as we rounded the next curve, I saw it: Melkøya, an island whose sole purpose was the drilling and shipping of natural gas.

It was a tiny disc of land, and steel buildings were jammed to its very edges. There was no organic matter in sight, just an industrial forest of oddly shaped structures. Large spires reached high above everything, spewing blooms of red flame and black smoke. Even in the darkness I could tell everything was in a palette of gray—snow and ice blanketing concrete and steel—and yet an electric radiance limned the island, warming it. Every light was set ablaze, making the place glow like a fiery and faceted ruby floating atop the dark purple of the Barents Sea.

How on earth would we ever sneak onto *that*?

I must've made some sound because Carden slid a hand from the handlebar to give my arm a quick squeeze.

The bike wobbled as he turned onto what I assumed was a driveway hidden beneath layers of ice and snow gone gritty and crusty with tire tracks and vehicle exhaust. At the end was a small white building glowing gray in the darkness. Crosses studded the surrounding snow.

"Creepy." I peered closer. It was a cemetery. "This is the safe house?"

"No," he said with a laugh, "this is Hammerfest Chapel. But the clouds are clearing, and I thought you might like to stop and see the lights." He got off the bike and nodded to the sky. "The view is good from here."

"Oh wow." The sky had taken on a strange cast, like I was looking through tinted glasses. A band of bright green flickered along the horizon. The northern lights.

I gave him an assessing look as he pulled a blanket from his pack. "Well aren't you prepared?"

He winked and snatched my arm, tugging me into the shadow of the church. "A man must have his priorities."

There'd been a day when such a statement and all it implied would've shot a bolt of heat through my very center. But I was here for a reason, and it wasn't canoodling with Carden under the northern lights, no matter how pretty they were.

I slowed down, pulling my arm back with the slightest resistance. "But...my mom. We're here for her."

He spread the blanket. "Aye, and so we'll get her. But nothing will happen tonight."

I crossed my arms at my chest. Nothing was going to happen—he didn't know how right he was. There was no way I could clear my mind of the single thought that'd taken hold: my mother was on that island. "I think I just want to get to the safe house. They're probably waiting for us, right?"

"We'll get there." He plopped down and patted the blanket

by his side. "But now it's evening, which means the day is only just getting started for the vampires."

"What does it matter?" I looked up at the sky. "It's dark. It'll still be dark in the morning."

"It matters to them. They have their habits." He leaned his elbows on bent legs, looking up at me. "Do you imagine they switch their routine with every vagary of the natural world? They're immortal—they'd go mad. No, if I know Jacob, they're sitting for dinner and a party." He reached up and tweaked my butt. "A party that would be greatly enhanced to discover a wee Acari bonbon like yourself. So sit beside me, love. Enjoy the lights. A spot of relaxation will help. I can feel your tension from here. Anyway, we'd be fools to attempt to broach the island before morning."

His words struck me as condescending, and I stiffened. "We'd be fools to not go to the safe house and get prepared."

He kicked back with a sigh. "You're missing the lights. And this chapel is the one part of Hammerfest that was spared during the war. The Nazis burned the rest of the town. Why not take ten minutes to enjoy it?"

Instinctively, I followed his line of sight, and it was my turn to sigh. The green lights had risen, swirling along the horizon like a cresting wave. "Fine. I guess you're right. I'm sorry...it's been..." I contemplated the last twenty-four hours—I'd been waterboarded by Fournier, pawed by Trainees, tossed into the sea—and decided it was no wonder I was feeling a little bitchy. I dropped next to him, leaning my head against one very broad, very strong shoulder. "It's been a really, really, really long day."

"Come, love. That's it." His voice was a low hum that seemed to reverberate through me, relaxing me. He wrapped an arm around me. A vampire's body was cool to the touch, but something about feeling so sheltered, so protected was enough to send a ripple of warmth through me.

Surely it was just stress that had me imagining distance between me and my vampire. I'd gotten so used to the bond, and now that it was gone, well, it wasn't bad, just different. Actually, it was probably good. Independence was, right? Of course I'd go through a period of feeling distant from him—the physical change alone would take time to adjust to.

We sat there for a while, and the tension slowly unspooled from between my shoulders; the looseness in my joints began to feel like something closer to my body's natural state.

I gave a little shiver, another sigh, and leaned all the way into him. "Do you ever get tired of being right?"

The brief spurt of optimism disappeared the moment we pulled our motorcycle in front of the safe house.

On instant alert, Carden tore off his helmet and put his finger to his mouth. With a slight tilt to his chin, he inhaled deeply, and a grim expression fell over his features. "I smell blood." In an instant, my stars were in my hand, but he shook his head. "No need. The only scent here is death. And yet"—he inhaled again—"go easy now."

Didn't have to tell me twice. It was pitch black now, and no lights were on in the house, either—it was merely a shadow standing in the darkness, the front door hanging open like a black, gaping maw. I pulled my flashlight from my duffel. Carden might've been able to see in the dark, but I wanted every crutch available.

I began a slow, silent approach to the door, sweeping the flashlight in front of me, my senses opened to the slightest movement or sound. I cast my light over the entryway path. Drifting snowflakes sparkled in the vivid circle of bright white. The ground glittered where the beam hit, bits of ice twinkling like so many tiny diamonds.

And then I saw the footprints. Red ones.

I squatted. "Someone," I whispered to Carden, "some

woman, walked out of here. Not very subtly either. She tracked a ton of blood." I stood, adding, "That was stupid."

"No, that was a *message*. For us."

"Do you think it was Charlotte?"

He shrugged and nodded to the house. "Let's see what else is waiting for us."

The front door swayed in the wind with a rhythmic *creak*. The only other sound was our breathing and the slow crunch of our feet on the snowy walkway.

Carden reached in carefully and flicked on the light, illuminating a scene of total carnage.

The place was small, more of a cottage than an actual house, and it was possible to take it all in with one glimpse. There was a kitchenette, a fireplace. A door opened onto a small bathroom, and I could spot chipped tiles, an ancient sink with hot and cold faucets, and a bare bulb hanging from the ceiling.

But the thing that snagged the entirety of my attention were the cots, four of them, arranged with military precision along the back wall. Gray metal frames bearing thin mattresses. And bodies. One per cot.

Blood, everywhere—smooth crimson pools of it shimmered on neatly swept floorboards, glistening in my flashlight's beam. I stepped closer, careful not to tread in it, and leaned down. A single set of footprints tracked in and out of the puddles.

Someone had gone from bed to bed, slicing throats.

I held my breath as I stood. Shone my flashlight on the bodies.

"Holy crap," I blurted. Because there was someone I recognized, someone whose white-blond hair was matted with blood. "What was Tracer Otto doing here?" My eyes shot to Carden. "I hated Otto."

"Aye, as did Fournier."

I gaped at him, my mind spinning. "Really?"

I'd known my world was complicated, but this was some serious up-was-down-and-down-was-up crap—where apparently my friend Josh was my enemy and the Tracer I despised had been an ally.

Disturbed, I found my gaze sliding from Carden. How could I know who to trust in this world, really, if it was impossible to genuinely know anybody?

Needing to fill the silence so he wouldn't somehow detect my thoughts, I said, "Who did this? Surely, Charlotte couldn't have gotten here so fast."

He pointed to a spot over the hearth, where a message was scrawled in blood,

Tick-tock.

XoX lottie

Her words echoed in my head: *I'll get to her first. You'll be too late to help your dying mommy.*

My eyes shot to his. "We have to go. Now."

I guess I'd expected him to protest, but for once Carden was in easy agreement with me.

"Aye," he said as he took my hand. "She can't be far ahead."

I got to the door first. Opened it. And immediately stumbled back a step.

A wall of men in uniform stood there, and for a second I thought police had come to raid the safe house. But then I made sense of the armbands they wore—red sashes, each with a white circle and a black swastika in the center.

CHAPTER THIRTEEN

"Freaking…what the…*Nazis*?"

Carden's arm reached around and slammed the door shut.

I gaped at him. Had I fallen and hit my head? Because this was seriously not computing. "Do those guys know what decade this is?"

"I warned you this was a bad idea," he said, and the nonchalant Carden-ness of it infuriated me, waking me from my stupor.

"Suddenly this is my fault?" I dashed to the window, peering out. I wasn't proud of how hysterical that'd come out. I needed to get a hold of myself and squinted out the window, trying to make sense of it all. Sure enough, their uniforms were tailored, every pleat sharp, every hat peaked and impeccable. These weren't costumes. "You didn't tell me there were Nazis."

"The Russians forced most of them out after the war. The rest went underground. You can imagine the Synod was only happy to take them in." He pulled his sword from the scabbard at his side.

"They have guns, Carden. You're bringing a sword to a gunfight."

He gave me a look, and there was something cruel in his eyes, there and gone in an instant. "Dismiss my blade, and you know naught of me."

There was a sudden chill in my hands, and I rubbed them together. "Just saying I wish we had more weapons." I plucked my stars from my boot, but how I wished I had that cool new boomerang star, the one currently stowed safely in my duffel... which was on the back of the bike. "The stupid duffels are still on the stupid bike."

He put a finger to his lips to silence me.

A stream of German came to us from the other side of the door. Things like *schnell* and *wie viele*.

My pulse hitched up a notch. I felt so naked—here we were, surrounded, and I had only four throwing stars. *Four*.

There was the misericordia, of course. That little nuke was tucked in my boot, but Ronan's warnings resonated in my head. *"You must keep it hidden. Even from Carden." Keep it hidden...from Carden...hidden...*

And then there was that look Carden had just given me—a strange electricity in his eyes that was giving me pause.

But those were Nazi vampires...just on the other side of this feeble structure. "Is this particle board?" I ran my hand along the wall. "What kind of safe house is this, anyway?"

"Hush, lass. They are many, but they are...different."

"I got that. They're *Nazis*."

"No. I mean they're a bit mad."

"Duh. Those dudes operated on schnitzel and rage."

I risked another peek outside. The vampires were circling, but not acting with particular urgency. There were eleven of them, and they knew they had us pinned and outnumbered.

Carden put a hand on my shoulder, and I must've jumped a

foot off the ground. "I mean the change left them a wee bit addled."

"Like Draug?" The only experience I had with such a thing were those Trainees who'd not successfully made it through the transition. They weren't dead, but they weren't exactly *compos mentis*.

"Not like Draug, either. Just a bit...obsessed."

"That doesn't make me feel better." One of them took a step closer to the house, and I let the curtain drop. "It's going to be a freaking siege," I said, lowering my voice even more. "I know history. Sieges aren't pretty. Neither are Nazis."

"Stop your panic," Carden murmured. "Freya's people keep weapons."

I had weapons, too. One very powerful one.

I thought again about busting out the misericordia. But Ronan, usually Mr. Man-of-Few-Words, had warned me, and in no uncertain terms. *"There might come a moment when your life hangs in the balance. If there is no other choice, if you wield this blade, you must do so swiftly and with confidence."*

I flexed my calf, reassured by the press of the cool silver against my skin. It would stay there until I really needed it.

"What do you mean they 'keep weapons'?"

He flung open a cabinet, tossing me a satchel. It landed at my feet with the unmistakable sound of wood clacking, heavy with stakes. "So we can stake them. What else kills vampires?" I began thinking aloud, and with a nod to his sword, said, "There's beheading. Light is uncomfortable."

As the words left my mouth, Carden handed me a metal box that looked like it'd been stolen from a student theater stage production. "UV spotlight." He tilted it, showing me a switch along the side. "Just don't aim the thing my way."

"Got it." I dumped out the stakes and tucked as many as I

could in my boots and up my sleeves. My weapons cache was scant but growing. "What else have we got?"

He opened another cabinet, and a bunch of useless crap clattered to the ground. He kicked through it and, with a slight shrug, tossed me an old garden spade.

"I thought this was a vampire safe house." I sneered at the rusty tool in my hand. "Am I supposed to plant tomatoes when we're done?"

"They like to eat." He plucked it from my hand and tucked it into my belt. "And you need every sharp-edged thing we can find."

Someone barked an order from the other side of the door. Feet stomped in unison.

"Ready?" Carden pulled me to my feet. "And don't say you were born thus."

The wink he gave filled me with courage. To him, this was child's play. He was so easy and carefree, and it was hard not to feel the same in his presence.

I squeezed his hand before I let it go. "Then let's just say you make me feel that way."

He nipped down and stole a kiss. And then he flung the door open.

They flew at us.

"Oh, crap." I stumbled backward and braced, waiting for those guns they had strapped at their sides to be unholstered. But they didn't reach for them. In fact, they pulled no weapons at all. They came at us, a swarm of blackened claws and shining fangs.

"The lamp," Carden shouted. His sword was out and he was stepping into the storm.

The UV thing. Of course.

"Watch out. On your left." I switched it on, and most of the vamps jumped out of the way of the superpowerful beam of ultraviolet light, but two didn't.

They caught fire almost instantly.

"Cool!" The light flickered off, and I shook the box until it flickered back on again, swinging just in time to flash another vampire rushing me from the side. "I'm loving this thing."

I stepped outside to find someone else to zap, but Carden snatched my shoulder and pulled me back. "It's safest inside. Stay in here as long as you can."

At my movement, a few tried to rush the door, including the guy I'd just blasted. Unlike the others, this one was still stumbling around, his face a charred black mask.

Resting the light on my hip, I grabbed a pillow from a nearby chair and shoved it at him, pushing him back out the door. "Oh no you don't." The fabric and feathers caught fire instantly, melting into his smoldering rib cage. He stumbled backward and fell, his entire body exploding into a cloud of embers and dust. "Three down."

I looked toward Carden, wanting to catch his eye in my moment of awesome, but he was too busy pushing past me, sword in hand. With one swoop of his strong arm, he beheaded two vampires who'd managed to enter through the window.

I jumped back. "Whoa. Thanks."

I spared Carden a quick look, then had to smile as I saw how fluidly he was dispatching the remaining vampires using just that one sword. He was hacking through them like a knife through butter, most beheaded, others run through. "You weren't kidding about your blade."

His answering laugh was carefree. The guy was enjoying himself.

I heard a knocking then the sound of shattering glass.

"In the back," Carden shouted to me.

"Got him." I dashed to where a vampire was crawling

through a window at the back of the house. "This has got to be the last of them."

I ran back, shining my lamp, which chose that very instant to flicker out. I shook it. It flickered on for a second, then died for good.

"Look out," Carden shouted, and when I looked back up, the vamp was right there in my face.

"Aw, hell." I gave the light box one last shake, then swung it up and caught the thing on the chin. His skin split and his chin smashed in, letting loose a stream of reddish black fluid.

I'd never get used to fighting other people, but there was something so unreal about fighting these monsters. Even their bloodshed was cartoonish and so completely inhuman.

Close-up like this I could smell him, and he smelled different than any vamp I'd ever met. He smelled *wrong*. And it wasn't the wrongness of the rotting Draug. This smell was pungent, fetid, like overripe fruit.

"Oh, sick." I swung again, and this time it was mostly to put something between me and the disgusting stuff spewing from his body.

He tried to speak, but it came out only as a wet, gurgling sound, followed by a breath of air. *"Hei—"*

Hi? Was he saying *heil?*

"Your guy lost, you *verrückt* Nazi freak." I hit him again, but the guy wasn't dropping. Adrenaline shot through my veins, making me tremble. I hit again, again, again, slamming the box against his stupid granitelike Teutonic jaw, but his chin only snapped back into place, presenting me with a gaping maw of a half-sneer.

He stepped forward and reached for me, and I was so taken aback by the strange robotic movements, he managed to grab hold of my throat before I could stop him. He grabbed and squeezed.

And squeezed.

Air was barely whistling through my constricted windpipe. In a second, it would close off for good.

I grabbed his wrists, but the entirety of my training came back and hit my brain with a dull thud. This was no way to save myself from being strangled.

I let go. My gaze went to his vulnerable parts—his eyes, his nose, his groin...but then I saw it, his *gun*.

I grabbed it from his holster. Put it to his forehead. And fired.

Nothing.

Then I panicked. I pulled the trigger again, and again, and each time there was just a lame little click. These Nazis had guns, but the last time they had ammunition was probably around 1945.

There was a shout from outside. Abruptly, his hands fell from my throat. He stood upright, clicked his heels together, and bracing his arms rigidly at his side said, *"Sieg heil."* Which, with his mashed up face, came out sounding more like, "Thig hi."

All the vampires I'd taken for dead had risen. As in, they just stood up. They stood and clicked their heels, a chorus of *heil* resounding around us.

"What the hell?" I looked back at Carden. "They're saying *heil*."

Two of the vampires I'd blasted with the UV light teetered in from outside, their skin gone, bones smoldering, eyes disappeared into empty black sockets.

I tossed the gun down. I had the misericordia—was now the time? Was this my life hanging in the balance? "How do we kill them?"

Carden nodded to the bodies lying behind him. The ones he'd beheaded and the one who'd exploded into embers were still down for the count. "We've got to take their heads, I imagine."

"You *imagine*? I thought you had the power of foresight. Shouldn't you have seen this coming?"

Five vampires remained standing, and their heels clicked again. The front door creaked, and in walked a vamp I hadn't seen before. He was dressed much the same as the others, but his long woolen overcoat announced him as their leader.

"Sieg heil," they all shouted. *"Sieg heil."*

Hail victory, hail victory.

I edged my way next to Carden and murmured, "I don't think so."

This was too weird. These dudes were clearly after us, but Carden had been right, there was something off about them. Like they were trapped in a film loop. They were soldiers enacting a siege, and yet they weren't completely seeing us, not really.

"Five injured soldiers and one general." I scooted close enough to Carden for our arms to touch. "And not a brain in the bunch."

The general began to speak, walking in front of the doorway with a sharp gait, unbending arms and legs moving at right angles. His words were all slurry, but my German was pretty good, and I managed to make out the words *"das Mädchen."*

The girl.

"I think they're talking about me. Do you think they can even—" I was going to say *understand* but five pairs of heels clicked as five sets of eyes landed on me.

"Damn," I whispered. "He's blocking the door. What now? We're stuck in here with them."

"Be easy, lass."

"Fine for you to say, you've got a sword. And I've got a shovel." I'd thrown my stars long ago.

Carden cut his eyes down at me. "You've got naught else?"

The misericordia. Was now the time?

But I knew it wasn't. I needed that to save my mother. If Carden and I couldn't figure out how to dispatch a few brain-damaged vampires who were stuck in the 1940s, well then, I sure wasn't going to be able to save my mom from Jacob's clutches.

"Yeah," I said, "I only have the shovel." And though that probably was capable of decapitating a vampire, it'd probably take me about five minutes of hard hacking. "But..." There was one thing in my possession, that wasn't the misericordia, able to decapitate these bastards.

"But?"

"The boomerang you gave me is in my duffel. I'd love to give it a test drive."

Carden glanced from the general guarding the front door and back to me. "And so you shall, love." He gave me a grin. "Go quick now, and I'll see to occupying their attention."

He didn't pause, he just leapt toward them, waving his sword. I heard a solid *thuck-thuck-thuck*. Three heads rolling.

"Jeez." I snapped-to and bolted to the door. "More warning next time."

The general was lunging at Carden, but another had taken his place at the open door, and his eyes were on me. "Crap." My hand went to the shovel tucked at my waist. "Stupid crappy shovel." It was all I had, but I guessed it was better than nothing.

I faked left and then bobbed around him, sweeping my shovel behind me as I passed, lodging it deep into his throat.

It wasn't a full-on decapitation, but it slowed the guy down enough for me to scramble out the door to the motorcycle. I ran, but the snow had been packed down by so many footprints, my feet slipped on the icy sheen. I slammed down hard onto my hands and sucked in a breath at the sharp pain shooting up my arms. Ignoring the icy grit ground into my shredded palms, I scrambled to get my feet back under me, then let momentum carry me, slipping and sliding to the bike. To my duffel.

Heavy breathing was coming up from behind me, a sort of gurgling hiss. And then another sound from the side, a whispered *heil, heil, heil.*

My body was shaking with cold and nerves, my palms bleeding, but I managed to open my bag. I shoved my hand in, and right away nicked my thumb on the razor-sharp edge of my boomerang. I pulled it out with a swallowed curse.

I saw now that two had followed me outside and they halted in their tracks, bodies gone completely still. Their eyes were pinned on my hands. On my bloody palms and thumb.

They were slavering, staring, with mouths hanging open. So creepy. And I wasn't about to wait for them to pounce.

"All right, boys. Here goes nothing." I hauled up my arm and slung the boomerang. At first I thought I'd messed it up—I mean, how stupid to think I could make the weapon work the first time I really used it in action? But as it spun through the air, I saw it was going to hit its mark. It sliced a throat, and I put up my hand to catch it, but the thing kept whipping around to slice the other guy's throat, and finally it whipped back to me, the flat side landing in my hand with the dull sound of a mallet on meat.

The two vampires teetered. Then dropped. Their necks were still attached to their heads, but barely.

"Holy shit." I shook my hand out—because *ouch* that stung —but even so, I couldn't help it. I had to laugh. "Holy shit that was *awesome.*"

And that's when I heard the clapping. An ironic slow-clap that I knew instantly wasn't Carden.

I dropped to my knees and pivoted around, poised for another attack. The boomerang was in my hand, sticky with blackish-reddish sludge, and I adjusted my hold. The steel was refreshingly cool in my sore palm. By the time I was cocking my arm to throw, not two seconds had passed.

But then my arm froze midair.

Two figures stood there. They wore long, dark cloaks with hoods deep enough to hide most of their faces. But the northern lights were high in the sky now and bright enough to cast an eerie greenish light along a nose here, a cheekbone there. Between the fineness of their features, the petite height of one, and the willowy silhouette of the other, I guessed they were women.

"Relax, Annelise. We are on your side." The smaller one pushed back her cowl, revealing a pair of upturned eyes and a sheet of long pale hair. I'd seen features just like this...on Sonja. "I am Freya and I think you know my pupil."

The tall one pushed back her hood. I did know her.

It was my old roommate. My nemesis. Drew Enemy Numero Uno. She'd tried to kill me. Hell, we'd tried to kill each other. Several times.

It was Lilac.

CHAPTER FOURTEEN

Lilac? *The* Lilac?

My mind spun. Lilac von Straubing.

I thought I'd finally succeeded in wiping her from the face of the Isle of Night. We'd battled to the death. I'd won. Tracers had come and scooped her away after our fight, and she'd never reappeared again.

Well, there had been a moment afterward, when I'd thought I'd spotted her at the last Synod summit. But I'd convinced myself it was my mind playing tricks on me.

Because Lilac? Alive? Impossible.

And yet here she was, the same old tall sip of bitch. At least now the annoyingly thick maple waves of her hair had been knotted into a prudish braid. She was watching me, her eyes glittering with hatred, an amused sneer tilting the corner of her mouth.

Slowly, I stood. I'd lowered my weapon arm, but I wasn't about to show them any weakness. "How did you escape? I thought I killed you."

"I knew you'd be happy to see me," Lilac said, and like

hearing a ghost from my past, the timbre of her voice flashed me back to a different time.

A time when Yasuo and Emma were alive. A time even before Carden. Before I'd understood the full horrific scope of this world I'd found myself in. Back then, I'd dreamed of escape. Hope was something that'd burned bright in my chest.

But my optimism had dimmed long ago—fighting Lilac to the death had been the first nail in that coffin.

She took an aggressive step closer, forcing me to crane my neck to look up at her. I gave her a quick shove, relishing the satisfying *oof* as the heels of my hands rammed just under her ribs. "A little personal space here."

Freya tittered with laughter. "Had I known there would be a kitten fight, I'd have sought you out long ago."

Was that a low laugh I heard from Carden behind me?

Screw this. Nothing riled me more than being patronized. I wasn't going to play this game. *Screw them.*

I looked back, and there was Carden, with just the slightest touch of amusement at the corner of his mouth. "Fine," I said to him. "You tell me. How did Lilac escape?"

Freya answered for him, every ounce of amusement gone from her voice. "Our friend Ronan has many uses."

Ronan? The sound of his name hit me like a cannon shot, and I had to lock my knees not to stagger. Ronan was a deep wound—one I'd been pretending wasn't there—and she'd just torn it back open.

The shock must've been clear on my face because Lilac gave a girlish giggle. She caught my eye and mouthed, *our friend.*

I let every ounce of loathing I felt seep into my voice, my eyes. "Glad I amuse you."

She gave me a sneaky little grin that made me want to claw her face off.

I had to resist taking a step toward her and satisfied my bloodthirsty urges with threats instead. "Don't make me kill you again, von Slutling."

I heard Freya's quiet laughter and gave myself a shake.

This was what the vampires wanted from us—catfighting and deadly childish antics for their endless amusement.

I needed to focus.

Ronan. He'd told me he and Carden were on the same side, but to hear this...that he'd saved Lilac, who'd wished me dead, whom he'd known I hated...I couldn't believe it.

I turned the full force of my anger on Carden, ready to give him what for, but he silenced me with a hard look.

"Caution, Annelise," he murmured in a voice absent of all sympathy. "She is my queen. And I'll brook no disrespect."

Freya was his queen. Something died in me as he said it.

She was his first priority. Carden would help me, but ultimately I was alone here.

Hell, I was alone *everywhere.*

Cool clarity washed over me. I'd obviously been alone from the moment I landed on *Eyja næturinnar* and I was doing just fine.

I was alive. I was a tunnel-ride away from my mother. And I was armed, like, in the biggest way ever. Not for the first time that evening, I patted myself on the back for keeping the misericordia hidden.

I sucked in a quick breath through clenched teeth. I could do this. I'd been taught disguise and deception by the best.

I put my hands up in surrender. "Yeah, yeah, I'm all kinds of respecting."

I'd made the words sound genuine, meanwhile I wasn't about to surrender. Or kneel to any queen. Or yield to any man, Vampire, Tracer, Watcher, Acari...*anyone.* And if Carden didn't know that, he didn't know me.

Freya tilted her head as she assessed me. "That was well done, child. And now I expect you to show your sister the same courtesies you show me."

"Sister?" I peered from Freya to Lilac, whom the ancient vampire seemed to be foisting at me.

She didn't mean *my* sister. That was absurd. For one thing, Lilac was, like, ten feet taller than me. There was no possible way we were related by blood. I must've missed something.

"Sorry," I told her. "I'm not following. Are we talking about Sonja?"

"No, we are not taking about Sonja," Freya answered cooly. "I said *your* sister. Or half-sister, if we're getting technical."

Her words, delivered with such casual cruelty, hit me like a punch to the gut. I could only stare. Surely, I wasn't hearing what my ears told me I was hearing.

"Shut your mouth before you catch something in it," Lilac said with a laugh. "You heard right, so just grow up and deal with it. I did. I mean, do you think I want to be related to *you*? Thank God we only share a father."

An absurd laugh escaped me, because into my mind flashed the image of my ne'er-do-well dad in Florida, Coors tall boy in one hand, remote in the other.

"No," Freya said, reading my mind. "The man who raised you wasn't your relation."

"I have a father?" My mind was reeling. First, I discovered a mother, and now I've got a dad out there, too?

Lilac was the one who replied, and with surprising vehemence. "No, we had a sperm donor. And he's long dead. We women aren't just more powerful—"

Freya finished the thought, drawing out the words, slow and meaningful. "We don't need men."

The words *tell me something I don't know* were on the tip of my tongue, but I knew better than to say that, considering my main hope for getting out of this alive had decidedly different plumbing than I did, and he was standing right next to me.

Having spoken of the devil, Carden spoke up with his customary nonchalance. "We're good for a few things, I think."

I ignored him, though. I even ignored the flirty light that'd briefly danced in Lilac's eyes at his words.

What was really going on here? Why was Freya here? If we're all one big happy family, might they help me? I'd assumed this was a suicide mission, but what if I was wrong? What if I didn't die at Charlotte's hand?

Hope. Might I find it again? Merely thinking the word was kindling the most fragile of embers in my heart.

As usual, where Lilac and I were concerned, it was the same planet, different world. I was thinking big picture, while she was still pouting at me, her mouth making a little moue of distaste. "I can't imagine being related to that bitch *you* call a mother," she muttered.

That tore me from my reverie. Had she met my mother? The thought that Lilac had gotten to see her before I did was too painful to contemplate.

I snapped, "Are you still talking?"

Lilac's own story came back to me in a rush, how she'd grown up with a foster sister in a well-to-do Connecticut suburb. Had she been a foster kid herself? On a hunch, I asked, "And I suppose you've met your biological mother, too?"

Freya put an arm around her and practically purred as she said, "Lilac is my creature."

"Your...your...? You and my mom both...?" I knew I was gaping, and I didn't have a chance to formulate any words before the ancient, ice-queen vampire was looking past me, already onto the next thing.

"Enough gossip," she said. "Time for business. Carden, when I heard you were coming, I couldn't believe it. It's always a pleasure to see you," she said in a voice so cool it was obvious it wasn't a pleasure at all. "Though I could've sworn I'd given you different orders. I only wanted female delegates at these festivities, and yet here you are."

My head swung to look at him. "Festivities?"

But he ignored me, telling Freya, "We came for the mother. You'd expressed an interest in her before."

I was on instant alert. *The mother.*

My mother.

Freya waved an impatient hand. "I know this. We've given up on Birgit."

Birgit? Was that my mother's name? The only photo I'd ever seen of her popped into memory...the long, strong legs and pale blond hair.

Birgit. Just sound of it propelled her from mother figure to beautiful Nordic badass.

"Is that her name?" I asked, instantly cursing the vulnerable hitch in my voice.

"Yes." Freya stepped toward me to cup my chin with an ice-cold hand. "And you are stronger than your mother will ever be. You get your power from both sides."

There it was. Back to this mysterious, promiscuous man who'd fathered me. "Was my dad, was he—"

"Vampire? No, child. A Tracer, long dead. But he'd been a man of great power." Still holding my chin in her cool talon grip, Freya directed her next words to Carden. "Which is why Jacob wants her."

Jacob. She'd pronounced it the German way, like *yah-cub.* Just as I'd heard it spoken when I'd infiltrated the Synod vampires before.

"So Charlotte was right," I said. "Jacob is the one who has my mother hostage." He was an ancient sexist asshat, and I'd take great pleasure in sneaking yet another prisoner out from under his nose.

But then another thought hit me. Charlotte didn't want to kill me. For her, this wasn't about my mother at all. This was her way to lure me to the island, to present me to Jacob.

And sure enough, Freya confirmed it as she said, "Charlotte toys with you, luring you onto Melkøya so that she might offer you on a silver platter to gain Jacob's favor. Now that Dagursson is dead, the little pest needs to find another bene-factor. But we can't let her give you away." Her fingernails curled into my skin as she pitched her voice to a creepy calm. "Not when I need you myself."

My every muscle stiffened, senses raw and ready. The only thing worse than needing a vampire's help was being needed by one.

The misericordia was practically pulsing in my boot now.

"And what better way to win Annelise's loyalty," Carden said smoothly, "than by allowing us to save her mother? Yes, it will throw her into Charlotte's path, but that poses no concern. Lottie is young and will be dispatched easily enough. It's past time that happened anyway." He shrugged, finishing with his usual studied nonchalance. "You said yourself you care naught for what comes of Birgit. So let us free her."

He was still ready to help me save my mom. Carden was still on my side. I stole a glance at him to detect the truth, get strength from it. But his expression was unreadable.

He *was* on my side, right?

Freya crossed her arms over her chest. "I said *we* don't need the mother. Jacob wants her, naturally. He needs all the females he can get. If you take Birgit from under his nose, he will see it as an aggressive act. An act of war." A look of distaste spread across her face. "And then my sister will get involved. She's been looking for an excuse to take me out and clinch her little fiefdom once and for all." She stepped closer, her delicate features crystallizing into something brittle and commanding. "No, we are here only for the celebration, as a courtesy. Not to stoke the flames of a battle we're not yet ready to fight."

That threw me. "Celebration? I thought this was a summit."

But Carden ignored me, giving Freya a casual shrug. "This fight, with the Synod, with the Directorate, has been long in coming. Does it matter if it culminates today or next year?"

Though his words posed a challenge, the way he stood there, like a soldier at attention, was far from confrontational.

"Yes." Freya's voice pitched suddenly deeper, until it became a low, cold hum vibrating painfully in my ears. "Yes, it matters. As does your submission. So you will stop this questioning. You will do as I command. And you will leave Birgit alone. She is a loss, but it's one we can afford."

"Not one *I* can afford," I heard myself say.

Apparently Freya heard me, too, because she swung on me, her eyes flinty with anger. Looked like I was no longer being ignored. *Great.*

"You will behave," she intoned, and I clutched my hand to my head, fighting the jaw-gnashing echo of her voice through my skull. "I will not see this precious balance undone. Not until we are stronger." At those last words, she gave me an assessing look, head to toe.

Like I might be just the thing to strengthen her.

I made my face go blank. Because over my dead body.

Her eyes narrowed to slits, almost like she'd read my mind. "Do as your vampire tells you," she said to me, "or I will change my mind about your future. And you won't like it."

My vampire? Something about the way she'd said it made it sound like I was his assignment instead of his girlfriend.

I cut my eyes to *my vampire*. He was standing at attention now, looking for all the world like her good little warrior.

"Enough bickering." She gave a quick clap of her hands, apparently done with this conversation. "I require a favor."

Carden tipped his head as he put a hand to his heart. "Yes, Mistress."

"I have an offering for Jacob's celebration. A gift to keep the peace. You will help our courier deliver it on my behalf."

He stiffened as she said it, and my mind went loopy to consider all the things someone like Freya might be giving to an enemy like Jacob.

I asked for the umpteenth time, "This one would still please like to know, what celebration?"

Lilac appeared at my side, leaning an elbow on my shoulder. "The Rising. The vampires meet, celebrate. Bleed powerful descendants like your mommy dry."

I flinched away. Carden hadn't told me that part.

"Oh yeah," Lilac said, seeing the horror on my face. "It's why Freya sent...*gifts*. It's them or us."

My chest constricted as it dawned on me what these gifts must be...or rather *who*. I whispered, "What the—"

Lilac curled her lips into a half-smile. "We're just looking out for number one. Lucky for you we're on the same side now, *sister*."

I didn't recall siding with anybody, thank you very much.

"Hardly." I rolled my shoulder, nudging her away.

I needed to focus instead on Freya and Carden, to pick this apart. What was going on and who were the players?

"But mistress, if I come bearing your offering, then everyone will know whom I truly serve."

"Are you not ready to profess your loyalties? This is the favor I ask. Not merely that you drive some ridiculous truck to Melkøya. I am telling you it is time for all my followers to turn their backs on Sonja and claim me as their true queen. The pieces are already falling into place on *Eyja næturinnar*. Soon Sonja will find she is standing alone on an island of sand, shifting perilously beneath her feet."

"What has happened on the Isle?" Carden asked.

"You will know soon enough. Now go to the Rising. Assist my courier. You will henceforth claim me as your one, true leader." Freya swung on me, and snapped, "And you. It astounds me that you're still alive." She thrust a hand toward me. "It's time."

I gave her outstretched arm a wary look. "Time...for what?"

"To come with me," she said impatiently. If ancient vampires could adopt a *duh* tone of voice, Freya just had. "We cannot allow Charlotte to find you. I will not let Jacob have you. My guard will escort you instead to my home on *Eilean Ban-Laoch*."

The night air was bitter cold, and yet I broke into a sweat, palms and pits going sour with panic.

Freya wanted to take me. I saw it in her eyes. And it wasn't just a whisk-me-to-safety thing, either. She wanted me to trade one island for another so she could keep me for her own, like a pet.

I'd disappear in a puff of smoke as yet another vampire took control of me.

Lilac grinned. "Say goodbye to your boyfriend." Her eyes were raking over Carden like maybe it might be her turn.

Thankfully Carden remained by my side, standing just as rigidly as I was. Frankly, I'd been wondering whose side he was on.

It gave me strength.

"I want to see my mo—" I began, but his hand on my arm silenced me.

"No," he said to Freya, and for an instant my heart swelled.

He was going to help me after all. But then he said, "Jacob already suspects our intentions. But how much will he appreciate your gift if he thinks you've brought him Annelise? She'll be our ticket inside. Her scent will ease our passage across the border. Once we're inside, I'll keep her safe and hidden. You will have the appearance of generosity and goodwill. Then, while your courier delivers the goods, I'll get Annelise off the island. She'll disappear, and you'll blame me."

Freya considered this for several moments. "I don't understand what is in it for you, Carden. Why keep the child close? What purpose does it serve you?"

He grinned. "Maybe I'm just a sentimental bastard."

But Freya didn't smile as she studied him. "You go to find the mother," she concluded with exaggerated disappointment. "After all I've said."

But Carden was undaunted. "You say you want to keep the peace, not endanger it. You need your courier to cross the border unmolested. You need Jacob to accept this year's offering. And I say, the merest whiff of Annelise will ensure safe passage. I do believe it is the best of all possible strategies."

Freya softened just the slightest bit. "I need your word you won't do anything foolish where Birgit is concerned."

He gave her a deep bow. "Please grant a faithful servant this one request."

Something in me relaxed just a little. I knew Carden. He was Mr. Honorable. And just now while he was fawning with loyalty, he hadn't explicitly given his word.

But then he added, "If you allow Annelise to see her mother —merely see—then she will go with you faithfully."

WTF? My mouth went dry. *I will?*

This was so not in the plan.

I began to protest, but there was a strange intensity to the look on Freya's face that kept me silent. She looked nervous. Anxious. Like she actually feared my rebellion.

Maybe I really was strong enough to get myself out of this. To get my *mother* out of this.

I'd pledge my loyalty, just as Carden did. But unlike Carden, when we reached the end of the game, I'd change the rules.

"Just this one thing," I pleaded. "Then I'll come with you."

Not.

Finally, Freya gave Carden a slow nod. "Fine. You will keep the child under wraps. Her scent will ease your crossing, but she is not to be seen under any circumstances."

Oh, I was going to be seen all right.

Because I had a goal. And it was very clearly different from their goal.

I was going to save my mother if I needed to kill Jacob and every Synod monster in my path to do it. Because I would get off this rock. Out of this *hemisphere*. Back to some sunny, hot place. Even stupid inland Florida would do.

My fury was ignited. And so was my hope.

CHAPTER FIFTEEN

"From now on, Carden McCloud, you will do as you're told." Freya snapped her hood back into place. "I must go. I've already wasted enough time. The courier will arrive within the hour. He will bring you to Melkøya. But first"—she shooed toward the houseful of dead Nazis—"you will clean up your mess."

The moment she and Lilac vanished into the night, I turned to Carden. "We're still going to save my mom, right? You were just placating her to keep me with you?"

He sighed, and it was a horrible, weary sound, like he was under siege from me or something. "Saving Birgit isn't out of the question," he hedged.

I opened my mouth to pick that statement apart, but he stopped me. "Don't say it. I'm doing the best I can for you."

The best he could for me. Because his very best was reserved for his own kind? I heard myself say, "You'll never leave her, will you?"

There was a horrible pause that told me more than any

words ever could. Finally, he asked, "Don't we have other concerns at the moment?"

I only shrugged. Carden was batshit loyal, and I knew I figured in there somewhere, but it was hitting me how I probably wasn't at the tippy-top of his list.

I swallowed my concerns. I was done playing their vampire games. I'd keep the peace and accept whatever help I could get.

After that, it looked like I'd be on my own.

Which meant I needed to harden myself even more. I needed to prepare. To get an idea of the full picture. Up till now, I'd let people like Carden and Ronan shoulder too much of the responsibility. But it was on me now to know everything.

As we headed back into the house to begin our vile cleanup, I changed the subject. "Please tell me this gift isn't what I think it is. I'd like to know what—or who—this courier is going to show up with." I couldn't control much in this world, but I could set my expectations.

The beleaguered look that washed over Carden's face told me all I needed to know. The gift would be exactly what I thought it was. Just one more horror in a spectacular canon of horrors.

And I'd deal with it like I always did.

"Never mind," I muttered. "Let's just get this over with."

I saw in Carden's eyes that he was done fighting—against this world, against me—and apparently I was done too, because we cleaned up in total silence after that, clearing bodies, stacking them in a frozen culvert, concealing them under a pile of icy branches and chunks of snow.

He speared his shovel into the newly formed snow bank and finally broke the silence. "We'll let Freya's people clean this up come spring. 'Tis their fault we were caught in a trap anyhow."

I didn't get a chance to reply before the sound of an engine carried to us through the still night.

My heart instinctively kicked into high gear. What hideous surprise was rattling up the drive?

I thought it and then it appeared, a tidy Euro-version of a box truck. It glowed white in the moonlight and was a bit dinged up, but it was the cargo space in the back that held my attention.

"What the hell?" I whispered to myself. I'd learned when I broke into the keep what the vampires craved. Whose hearts they consumed in order to transition from Tracer to Vampire. Whose blood they drank to sustain them.

I'd suspected what Freya's offering would be, but seeing that cubelike cargo area—large enough for boxes...or bodies—brought home the truth.

As the truck shuddered to a stop, Carden walked straight for the back, and I was right at his heels. After a few sharp slaps of his hand, he unlatched the door.

I stood beside him. I had to see for myself.

It creaked open. And sure enough, over half a dozen girls were inside. Their bleeding bodies littered the floor, lying atop a tarp. Gotta keep the vehicle clean, right?

"I'll get her for this." I clenched my jaw thinking of Freya, of her betrayal of her own sex, and I had to choke back the sudden clench of emotion in my throat. "These are just girls."

I could tell from the softer, younger features of a couple of them that they were brand-new Acari. But there were older girls, too. There was a tangle of blue-catsuited legs belonging to a couple of Guidons and one Watcher. Then I saw two faces that sent a stabbing pain through my chest.

My old proctor, Kenzie, was there. She'd once saved me from attack when Yasuo had lost his mind in a late-night pool-side showdown. And there was Regina, too—the petite, curly-haired Acari whom I'd come to consider a bit of a protégé. Ronan had recently saved her from bullying in the dining hall, but it hadn't been enough to rescue her from *this*. The Isle of Night was rich with bullshit irony like that.

It was like a veil of red dropped over my eyes, because the next thing I knew, I'd leapt into the back of the truck and was on my hands and knees in front of her.

As my eyes adjusted to the dark space, I detected a fine thread of steam puffing from her nose with every exhale.

I gasped. "She's alive." I scampered from body to body. They had varying degrees of injuries, but every single girl was breathing. "All of them. They're alive."

"Aye, they're Freya's wee gifts." Carden's voice was thick with scorn. "Come, love." He put his hand out for me to take. "Best you ride up front."

His scorn wasn't enough. Judgment wasn't nearly enough. This situation demanded more.

I clambered closer but ignored his outstretched hand. I hissed, "We have to help them."

I expected outrage from Carden or even sympathy, but the expression that met mine was hard and as cold as the polar night air. "Get out of the truck, Ann."

My jaw, my stomach, my heart...it all fell in disbelief. "You're going to allow this?"

He snatched my arm and practically dragged me back out of the truck. "What would you have me do? You ask too much already. You cannot have your every whim met. Some things are not possible, Annelise." He slammed the door shut and relatched it. "They aren't pure of blood. We could save them, and then what? They're weak. These are the girls who have failed. Sonja wanted their hearts, which would've been a fate far worse than this. But they were salvaged—at great risk to Freya's operatives on the Isle—and would you make *their* risk count for nothing? Think of these as sacrifices. For a greater good."

"Who are you right now? I can't believe what I'm hearing. They're not sacrifices, they're *girls*."

"You know well who I am. *What* I am. And what of you, Annelise? Are you so innocent?" His expression softened. "My love, please listen. This is a dangerous game we play. We are in deep. And we cannot lose. If Jacob and his people win, the consequences would be dire indeed. This"—he hitched a thumb toward the truck—"would be nothing compared to the carnage that the Synod wants to unleash."

"I know, but..." I deflated, my voice tapering out. "It's Regina..."

"I love you, Ann. God help me, I am yours to command. You want to save these girls? Fine. I will kill the courier myself. But—" He stressed the word, reaching for me, and this time I let him take my hand. "—You wish to see your mother, correct?"

At my pained nod, he went on. "Then you must choose. Because if these girls aren't delivered on schedule, then you'll not get even the slightest glimpse of Birgit. Because the vampires will be raging. *Freya* will be raging. What do you think will happen when she goes before Jacob to pay her obei-sance and her offering doesn't appear? She may want you on *Eilean Ban-Laoch*, but even that would be too great a transgres-sion for her. If you took this from her, she'd find you and use *you* as a token of her respect instead."

He took my shoulders, holding me tightly. "I will not let that happen. I will bring you inside because I love you. Because it is what you desire. You *will* look upon your mother. But this" —he spared a quick glance into the back of the truck—"this is too great a risk. To me, you are worth an entire truckload of girls."

"But I'm not. I'm just me. Why should I be more important than anybody else?"

"You are," he said fiercely. "You wee fool. Have you not figured it out? Your blood, and yes, even Lilac's blood, it's richer. Closer to those of our ancestors. It's why you've always been stronger than the others. Why Alcántara wants you alive. Why Sonja wants you dead. Your blood would reinvigorate their stock. And it would certainly be more than enough to buy another year of peace between Freya and Jacob. It'd give us another year to gather our strength. To build our army. Because this is a war we fight, Annelise. And these girls, yes, I know it's hard, but these girls are a small loss in a single battle, when what we fight is a war. A war that's spanned centuries."

I wanted to believe him. To feel in my heart what he felt. I wanted to stand tall with Carden by my side. But how could I when this was his worldview?

His voice gentled. "Listen, dove. Our world is not black and white. It's never so easy as that. Not even when I walked this earth as a man was the world that simple. Don't forget the good Freya has done. How she saved me. Spared me that I might care for my family."

He was entrenched, and there was no getting him out. Not so long as he pledged himself to Freya. I swayed into him. "I just wish things were different."

Carden shifted me so that he could catch my eye. "I work for Freya. Like it or not, you do too now. I know it's hard to accept, but trust me when I say she is the lesser of many evils."

He was kneading my shoulders in a way that was supposed to reassure me, and ever so subtly, I found myself receding from his touch. "You're right. We can't let Jacob win. It's just... this isn't my war."

"Aye, love. But it's mine."

I put on my game face. Gave him my accepting nod. But

inside I grieved. I railed. Because I did not accept this. Would not.

I'd save my mother and then I'd run as far and as fast as I could from here. And if they killed me...well, anything would be better than living among this evil. Because once this war was fought, I was sure there'd be another, and another, and another. That's just how it was with creatures who craved power as these vampires did.

"Okay," I said, letting him steer me toward the front. "I get it. But I don't have to like it."

"And I do?" Carden mused, but his usual cavalier humor rang false in my ears.

I kept my eyes to the ground as I tried desperately to arrange my features into something brave. Something cold and strong and standing alone.

There was the creak of cold metal as Carden opened the passenger door. He greeted the driver. "So you're the new errand boy."

I looked up.

Behind the wheel was Ronan.

CHAPTER SIXTEEN

I staggered backward and bumped into Carden, who caught me by the shoulders. "Get in," he said, jealousy pulling his voice taut. "I'll padlock the back."

My vampire wouldn't like seeing Ronan affecting me this way.

But affect me he did. Betrayal seared through me at the sight of him.

I understood why Carden was here. I got his motivations. He was a *vampire* in the midst of a war. He was a creature of honor and loyalty who owed a debt to someone he called his queen.

But Ronan? Ronan was my friend. Probably my best friend. Often my only friend. He had a heart—an actual live, pumping one. He'd always been...well, he'd been my hope. The one ray of light that'd kept me alive, literally and figuratively.

His presence here was incomprehensible.

The deception, the agony of it, slammed into me like a physical thing that wedged deep under my skin, wending through me until the feeling lodged somewhere in the vicinity of my heart and made it hard to breathe.

Seeing Ronan behind the wheel of that truck threw everything I knew, everything I understood about myself, into doubt. My friendships, my trials, my triumphs...none of it meant anything if Ronan was actually this person. This person who could drive a truckload of girls—girls he'd *taught*—into the enemy's innermost lair, serving them up for this absurd vampire celebration like they were a selection of canapés.

"I guess I shouldn't be surprised," I said, not bothering to mask the venom in my tone. "I hear you're the one who saved Lilac. You remember her, right? The one who kept trying to *kill me?*"

I climbed into the truck and dove straight for the back cab area, clambering onto the tiny bench that served as a backseat. Being in this close a space with him was bad enough—I couldn't bear if I had to sit next to him.

I adjusted myself on the hard, narrow perch, and tore into him. "But I guess that's what you do, right? Run errands for vampires. *Serve* them. Maybe it's Sonja, maybe it's Freya—does it really matter as long as you make it out alive? I guess this is who you've really been all this time."

Still no reaction from him, so my voice rose in intensity. I was letting it all out, all the terror and heartbreak that'd built up during my time on the Isle, I let it all rip. "All your talk of caring about me, looking out for me, it's all been bullshit. Pretending to be sad when you lost your so-called friends— remember Amanda? Tracer Judge?—it was so perfect how you pretended to be *so sad* when they were killed, but they're the ones who died, right? Not you. Because you never risked anything. Because all this time you've been this...this...*person* who throws girls into the big old vampire wood-chipper, and then afterward you pull out the ones who are still breathing and take them to where they're needed most. Supper's on, right?"

He was silent. But I needed him to talk, dammit, so I pressed, "What are you even doing here? You knew I'd be here. Aren't you ashamed to show yourself in front of me? Why did you come?"

He turned, and damned if I hadn't situated myself too close. His face was inches from mine, his words exploding in a tormented rasp. "You think I'd really just let you go?"

The earnestness, the anguish in his voice was a fresh spear through my heart. Because I knew now.

It was all a lie.

Carden swung his large body into the passenger seat, and I flinched away so abruptly, I thumped my head on the back of the tight space. "Dammit," I hissed.

He looked from me to Ronan, and something like distrust sharpened his features. But then he slammed the door and kicked back in his seat like he was on a chaise in the South of France instead of a box truck headed for an industrial island infested with ancient evil.

"Did you have any trouble?" he asked Ronan.

The Tracer gave a tight shake to his head.

The truck rumbled back to life. Ronan put it in gear and put the safe house behind us.

There were a few beats of silence before Carden, sounding impatient, pressed, "You can't tell me Fournier just let you go."

"Fournier is dead," Ronan said curtly. "Alcántara is in charge."

A bark of a laugh escaped Carden. "That sop?" Then he was instantly serious. A muscle in his cheek twitched. "Not for long. Not if I have anything to say about it."

"What does that mean?" I asked, but I knew. There'd been a time when Carden's words would've upset me, or confused me, or worried me for his safety. But now they only shored up this wall I was rapidly constructing around my heart. It was always going to be some battle or other with these guys.

"So Fournier is dead, huh? And the Spaniard finally found the spine to make his move." Carden stared out the window, contemplating. "Fournier, dead. Dagursson, dead. All we need to do is dispatch Sonja, and once more we shall claim *Eyja næturinnar* for our own."

Ronan only nodded.

In a move I was sure had been cultivated to annoy, Carden reached over and jostled his shoulder. "You seem tense, pup. What's your concern?"

Without looking at me, Ronan twitched his head ever so slightly toward me. "It's not safe for her."

Fresh outrage erupted like lava in my belly. I was so not about to be discussed in the third person.

I craned my body forward to the very edge of the bench seat. "So *that's* why you came? To stop me? Because you think I'm weak? Or are you just scared I might hurt your sister?"

Ronan's face was like granite, but those haunted green eyes flicked to the rearview mirror and locked with mine for the space of two heartbeats.

He looked back to the road and said flatly and simply, "There's a cloak on the floor. Put it on. Cover yourself with the blanket. When we reach the tunnel, you must hide as best you can. I don't want you with the others. It's too dangerous."

"*Now* it's too dangerous?" An exasperated breath puffed from my mouth in a cloud of steam. "Fine. Whatever. You boys clearly know what you're doing."

I settled myself under layers of fabric, muttering curses with every bump and jostle of my body against the hard bench. I focused on the sound of the truck's shifting gears.

We slowed. There was a jarring *thud-thud-thud-thud* as the

wheels clattered rapid-fire over what sounded like metal bars set in the tarmac.

Sound began to echo differently. Electric light sliced into the truck, strongly enough to glow amber through the layers of fabric covering me. Ronan sped up again.

We were in the tunnel.

After a few minutes, there was an explosive burst of air outside the truck and I was shrouded once more in blackness.

Out of the tunnel again.

We gradually slowed to a stop. Ronan unrolled his window, and a deliciously fresh breeze rushed into the cab, carrying the loud caws of sea birds. There were shouts, too, and I strained to make sense of voices calling out in German, English, some Nordic languages, too.

A male voice was suddenly right there, loud and speaking to Ronan at the window: who was he, what was in the truck, who sent him, what was his affiliation?

Carden began to speak, but a thickly accented voice stopped him. "Not you. We want to hear what this human has to say for himself."

As Ronan delivered his answers—delivery...offering for the Rising...for Jacob...I serve Freya.

It was probably the first time he'd publicly claimed to side with her instead of Sonja, and while I might've been pissed at him, I had to give him props for courage.

But the sentry wasn't so impressed. He peppered Ronan with more questions, and as the Tracer replied, he pitched his voice in a subtle extension of his persuasive powers.

But it didn't work. The male voice grew tense.

I was taking only shallow sips of air now, petrified that this guard who stood a mere foot away from my head might detect me.

They sounded increasingly strained as the interrogation

went on. Yes, Ronan knew Sonja. As did Carden. No, Ronan was simply a courier. Yes, he'd spent time on *Eyja næturinnar*. Yes, just a courier.

"A dumb courier who knows nothing," Carden interrupted.

"Oh, I wouldn't say that," a female voice cut in.

I sucked in a breath and held it, nails cutting into my palms. Because I recognized that voice.

"This is no mere courier. Brother dear, how lovely you could join us."

It was Charlotte.

CHAPTER SEVENTEEN

"Lottie," Ronan said.

Not Charlotte. Not crazed-vampire-shrew. But his old nickname for her. *Lottie.*

How terribly sweet.

The feeling of being double-crossed, of being lied to, betrayed, and stabbed in the back by the one person I'd thought I could trust bloomed anew, turning my stomach, making me feel like I might puke in the back of this stupid truck.

"Did I hear you say you bring gifts from *Freya*?" she purred. "How very curious. That could only mean you've switched sides. I didn't know you had it in you. I mean, who'd have guessed that a pair of brass balls came with the pretty face?"

From the sounds in the front seat, it seemed like he flinched from her. "Oi, girl, hands off."

Charlotte giggled.

My cheeks were damp, and I hated myself for the tears I realized were falling. Because it was a regular family reunion up front, what with Ronan clowning around with his sister...

whom he almost certainly knew wanted me dead. Just as Lilac had wanted me dead. Lilac, whom he'd rescued from *Eyja næturinnar*.

It was becoming completely clear just how little I actually knew Ronan. His voice was light, speaking with his sister, and the sound of it made me feel like the loneliest person in the world.

"And look who you brought," Charlotte chirped. "Carden McCloud. Please tell me this is *my* gift." She tittered some more. "So Carden, you've sided with Freya, too? It's not like you to be so bold with your alliances."

A guard called out, his voice shifting as he spoke to someone behind him. "It's McCloud."

What had I thought? That we'd sneak in, I'd save my mom, and sneak back out? Stupid. They'd all warned me how dangerous this mission was. I'd been stupid and stubborn not to listen. Because apparently Carden was the only thing standing between me and Charlotte, and things weren't exactly looking great for him.

Ronan was all business as he said, "Just let us pass, Lottie." I heard another rustle as he shifted, probably checking his watch, because he added, "It's getting late. Jacob needs what's in this truck as soon as possible. So if I were you, I'd expedite this, aye?"

"It'd be no good for anyone if these goods were to spoil." Carden sounded like he'd casually leaned across the cab to say it.

Spoiled goods. That's what we were to these vampires. Goods, then spoiled goods. The concept was so repellent, I shrank into myself even more. Would that I could shrink into nothing and just disappear.

The sentry, further away now, said, "Jacob is occupied and doesn't give two shites about your goods."

"It's true." Charlotte sighed, sounding bored. "Jacob is busy interrogating Sonja. She's being asked to...explain herself. In fact, it's very lucky for you two that you've decided to question your loyalties. It's not a good time to be allied with her. Everyone who does seems to end up dead. Jacob thinks she's lost control of her little kingdom."

Banging on the passenger door startled me, and I almost gave myself away by flinching.

"Och, lad, cool your jets." Carden's usually easy confidence sounded strained. "The Rising is a joyful time. The cargo is never checked. What's this then?"

"You been under a rock?" another voice asked. "The coup on Sonja's territory means heightened security for us."

"Which raises a very interesting question," Charlotte said. "I wonder if we can trust you, Carden. Your timing does seem very convenient."

"He's with me," Ronan said tightly.

"Yes, well. You've shown bad judgment before."

"Time for you to get out, McCloud," the sentry said.

But Carden only laughed. "You wish to unload the cargo here?" He'd laced the words with playful disbelief.

Oh, Carden. I'd been so annoyed with him, with his overbearing ways, but now he was *my* Carden. He was doing all he could to protect me, but what was this forced nonchalance costing him?

"I'd get out if I were you," Charlotte said lightly.

"Now, McCloud."

Carden whispered under his breath, an anxious *shite* that made sweat break out in cold pinpricks up my spine. But when he opened the door, he was all calm and casual. "How might I be of service, lad?"

Another voice burst in now, ragged and accented, accompanied by a hand slamming the hood. "Take him."

There was a shout. Carden cursed.

Then a male voice in a close snarl, "I'll know where your true allegiance lies if I have to torture you for the next five hundred years."

At least I thought that was what he said. I could barely make out the words through the sound of my heartbeat thundering in my ears. Dread was pumping through my veins, making my insides feel thick and slushy, chilling me to my core.

There was a scuffle.

"I can do it," Carden snarled inexplicably, and I was desperate to see what was happening.

Was Carden pulled from his seat or did he get out himself? Either way, I felt his sudden absence like a cold, black hole. I no longer even had our bond to strengthen me. Without him, I wouldn't survive. There were just too many of them. What had I been thinking trying to sneak in here?

My hand was resting on my boot. The misericordia. I could use it. I could kill everyone in my path if it came to it. It'd be suicide, but at least I'd be bringing as many of these monsters down with me as I could.

"Now the only thing missing is that little pet you share." Charlotte sniffed and sniffed again, then said with exaggerated wonder, "Or *is* she missing?"

I was a sitting duck back here. Why wasn't Ronan speaking up? He could've created some diversion. Was he going to just let this happen to me?

The reality of my situation hit like a massive, bitter-cold wave, smacking me. Rolling over me.

Everyone had told me all along just how valuable my blood was, and I'd refused to listen. Even Charlotte had warned me, dared me. But she'd have known. She'd have been waiting for me. Now I'd be dragged into these festivities, drained dry. My heart served up on a platter. And that would be that.

Game over.

"Did you bring me a present, brother?" Charlotte sniffed again, more deeply. Something poked my leg. "Ooh! What have we here?"

I was dragged out by my foot, unceremoniously pulled from the back and hauled out the passenger-side door. I'd tucked my chin at the last moment, but I landed awkwardly, on my side, and my skull hit the tarmac hard.

"Careful not to kill her," was all Ronan had to say about it. "Her blood is too valuable."

Careful not to kill her. That was it. Not a peep more.

I heard him get out of the car, and I was letting the tears flow now. It wasn't even the knowledge that I was headed to my certain death—I'd been expecting that since I'd landed on the Isle of Night.

I cried for the loss of Ronan. Who I'd thought he was. Who I'd thought I was to him.

I was lonelier than alone. I was utterly bereft. I had nobody.

There was my mother, I supposed. Though she was surely beyond my reach now. And anyway, who knew who she'd be? Who knew if she ever even spared me a thought?

All I knew, all I had, was this very moment, and at this very moment, nobody cared.

Even Carden—he might've stayed and thrown himself between me and the guards, but I knew with certainty, he'd be measuring his options until the bitter end. Weighing my life against the greater cause. He'd said it himself: *these girls are a small loss in a single battle, when what we fight is a war.*

And what was I? Just another girl, after all, in a series of girls over centuries.

Well, screw that. If I was going to go down, I'd go down swinging.

I wiped my eyes and felt blood and tears smearing across my face. I rolled to my feet, then popped up.

Ronan was instantly by my side. For a second, my heart swelled to think he'd changed his mind. That this surreal and horrific abandonment was just some terrible misunderstanding.

We were a team again.

But when I bent to pull the misericordia from my boot, he swept his hand out and grabbed my arm, jerking me so hard my head whipped sideways. His fingertips were bruising, curling to the bone.

"No," he growled, and then a surge of power hit me. I'd experienced his abilities before, but not like this. He blasted me with his power, and I couldn't move. For a few seconds, I couldn't even breathe.

It surged through me—his will, his persuasion—but this time, I felt something more. A cacophony of intense emotion roiled from his hands and shot through me in bolts of excruciating pain. Light exploded in my head.

It was too much. This was a violation.

It was unbearable. Was this a flash of the true Ronan? It was fury. All chaos and white noise.

I stumbled back a step and had to wipe my eyes to see. My mouth was suddenly full of too much saliva, and convulsively, I swallowed and swallowed again. I refused to gag like a sick child in front of these monsters. "Don't...do that...again."

But he did grab me again, and I glared at him. Power was pulsing from him, shivering over my skin, and I shook it off. Shook him off. "I said, stop it."

"Lovers' quarrel?" Charlotte had appeared at my shoulder.

"He's not my lover," I snapped.

"Is he not?"

I turned to him. I raked him up and down with my gaze. In my heart, I said my final goodbye.

I thought I knew him, but I'd been so, so wrong. He'd never been my friend; he'd always only been in service to the vampires. From the first moment I set eyes on him—this had been one long betrayal.

Steadily, coldly, I said, "I could never love someone like him."

"Truly?" Charlotte stepped closer and peered from him to me and back again. She tilted her head, studying him with a little *tsk-tsk*. "Poor little Ronan. Nobody ever did love you back."

What did she mean? I stared at him, willing him to look at me, but he'd turned away and refused to meet my eyes.

Charlotte turned to the guards, and in a brisk voice said, "Take my brother. I've decided he can't be trusted." She snapped her fingers at me. "And bring her in with the offering. She'll round out Jacob's feast nicely."

CHAPTER EIGHTEEN

I was the first girl they dragged inside. It took two guards, and if I hadn't been trailed by a dozen others dragging nearly as many Acari behind me, I could've gotten free. These guys were strong, but they weren't Vampire—more like a Synod version of Tracers. That I was denied the opportunity to bring them down frustrated me beyond endurance. Instead, I had to satisfy myself with dragging my feet as I busted out every curse I could think of, in four different languages.

But that was me being stupid and childish again—a road I'd been walking for almost two decades and probably what had gotten me into this situation in the first place. It was time to grow up, I chided myself. *Reborn, remember?*

Being reckless wouldn't get me out of this mess. Being smart would. Smart and strong.

I still had fight in me—I was far from done. And, ironically, it'd been vampires who'd trained me for just this situation.

I focused on my breath, forcing my heartbeat to slow. As we walked, I turned my attention to the factory itself. It was a warren of pipes and hallways in a palette of white and black and gray. The only pops of color to be found were on the occasional warning signs scattered throughout, with admonitions in Norwegian to *Beware* and *Keep Out.*

There were workers around, too. Not many, but they were a grim lot—all human, decked out in crisp coveralls and hardhats.

So, it was a working factory. Which meant those pipes had natural gas running through them. I made a mental note, just in case I needed to blow this place off the map.

Which I'd never do, I realized—not with all these human workers inside. I'd been changed by the vampires, but not that much. I refused to become a monster myself. It was an attitude that could very well kill me, but the reborn part of me—that lone, hard kernel of Annelise I shielded like a sputtering candle flame—thought that was okay.

For a while, I managed to keep track of where we were going, constructing a mental map in my head. But the longer we traversed the labyrinth of colorless hallways, the more I lost my bearings.

By the time we reached the freight elevator, I was completely turned around.

I hesitated upon seeing it. It was one of those old-fashioned lifts with scrollwork and smoked mirror paneling, and I knew by now how old-fashioned things generally lead to old-fashioned bloodsuckers.

But the guards shoved me in, stabbed the door-close button, and we went down. And down. There was a little click and flash of light with each floor we passed, and I counted up as we descended. When we finally got off, we were five stories underground. I pushed from my mind the thought that this meant we were as many stories beneath the sea.

I was taken to a dimly lit dining room, and it was a jarring departure from the antiseptic brightness of the factory. Here, there was neither a human face nor hardhat in sight.

Instead, rich, velvety brocades draped every surface. Candelabras were scattered about the room, resting atop thickly carved side tables. Arrangements looking like they'd been pulled straight out of a Baroque painting had been placed around the room, featuring dozens of dark roses, their scent hanging heavy in the air, plus bowls of fruit, decanters, a few skulls.

Nice.

Did I just say that out loud? *Crap.* I think I said it out loud, because about half a dozen pairs of cold, dead eyes slowly turned to me.

Vampires—of the old and craggy Dagursson variety—were lounging in upholstered chairs around a table on which a massive feast was spread. The Synod of Seven, I presumed. And, I noted with some interest, they were all men. Female vampires were more powerful than their male counterparts, so why the testosterone fest?

They all wore the same thing: monklike cloaks with hoods pushed back and sleeves that drooped as they drank from chalices of something that might've been wine or blood. An empty chair was set between each one, and it didn't take a rocket scientist to guess who the guests of honor were going to be.

Seven vampires, seven empty chairs. This had *last stop* written all over it.

Rough hands grabbed me from behind and foisted me toward the table into a seat.

Next to Jacob.

Ancient German monk, sadist, and ballroom dancing enthusiast. I'd know Jacob anywhere. It was in one of his dungeons that I'd first met Carden, so long ago now. I'd dressed up like a maid and rescued my Scottish vampire from under his nose—a fact which, I'm sure, hadn't exactly made Jacob my greatest fan.

"I see the girl who pretended to be a scullery is actually one of the true blooded," he said in his thickly accented voice. He steepled his fingers as he stared at me. "How wondrous that you stumbled into my little web. They claim you are smart," he added with a wry smile, "but it seems to me you've been more lucky than bright."

I'd show him lucky.

But I made myself school my features. I wasn't going to be reckless Drew any longer.

His attention went back to the door and he snapped his fingers. "Quickly, quickly now."

One-by-one, the other girls were led inside. Kenzie and Regina, a Watcher named Clara, two Guidons, and two new girls.

A cold plume of dread spiraled through my belly. There were eight of us. And there were seven chairs.

"Stop," Jacob commanded. He rose and stepped to the girls, who were barely standing, slumped against their captors. Slowly, he went one by one, inhaling deeply the neck of each captive. He paused at one of the new girls—so new, I didn't even know her name. "This one is expendable."

I hopped to my feet. "Wait—"

But it was no good. One of Jacob's lackeys slashed her throat without hesitation.

I was shaking as I dropped back into my seat. The other girls were led to their own chairs, where they all slumped, looking catatonic, obviously drugged.

I sent up yet another silent curse at Ronan. How could he betray us like this?

"Surprised to see your friends?" Jacob's aged skin pulled into countless wrinkles as he focused on me, studying me. "Or, wait. Are they your friends? I was under the impression that you had none. Well, there's Carden, I suppose." He waved a dismissive hand. "But he's being taken care of."

Carden. I'm the one who got him into this. And he was suffering for it.

The misericordia pulsed in my boot. Time telescoped, and suddenly, I knew—everything I'd endured, every move I'd made, every decision, it'd all lead to this moment.

I would stake Jacob.

His death might not take down the entire Synod, but it sure would cripple it in a major way. The power vacuum on the Isle of Night was nothing compared to what would happen if I were to rid the Synod of its leader. The impact would reverberate across all the isles.

Could I do it?

I hardened myself just a little bit more. I'd sensed I was a goner when I stepped into that elevator, but contemplating one's own death was one thing—it was quite another to run headlong toward it.

I cut a look at the old monk. I could do it, and I would. But I needed to act decisively. I was out of options—it was time for the *run headlong* stage of this game.

And if it saved just one of my friends, it would be worth it. If I didn't make it out—and I probably wouldn't—I had to believe my mother would've been proud. If I truly was her daughter, she'd want this bastard taken down once and for all.

"Carden means nothing to me," I lied. To stake Jacob, I needed to get close, and I scooted my chair until it abutted his.

His eyes widened in surprise. "I'm glad to hear you say it. He has been a thorn in my side. Now that he's been taken care of, it will be a pleasure to"—his gaze strayed to my neck and lingered there—"sample the storied Annelise."

Repressing a shudder, I leaned on the arm of my chair. I let my hand graze his.

I had nothing to lose. Nothing.

And nothing would be accomplished by half-measures. If these ancient asshats thought they were getting some hapless teenager, then that was what I'd give them. Let them think I was a fool. I'd been a fool in truth for so much of my life anyway. Time to capitalize on my biggest talent.

I leaned back in my chair and gave him my blandest expression. "This is all very Medieval."

One of the vampires overheard and shot me an incredulous glare. "Would you like to lie upon the table that we might pry open your ribs and feast?"

"Ignore her," Jacob said to his companion. "Annelise merely toys with us. Don't you?" He reached a cold, clawlike finger to touch my cheek, tracing slowly down my jaw. "You're a clever one. All the better to build my clever army, nurtured by your blood."

A commotion at the door drew everyone's attention. A female captive was being dragged inside the room. Two figures held her, and I could tell by a flash of fangs that they were vampires, brawny ones—which meant she was important. She was small and slim, and her long, hooded robe told me she was Vampire, not Acari.

Her head lolled, and a sheet of long hair spilled from her hood. The shade, the texture, it was as familiar to me as my own.

CHAPTER NINETEEN

My nonchalant mask dropped and I gasped. "Is that...?"

"Is this...?" Jacob peered at me, reading my expression, then back to the hooded figure. "Ah! You think this your mother." He clapped once, his laugh a sudden bark. "No, our Birgit has grown too weak. She no longer needs shackling." He watched me, keeping that amused grin on his face, and let the silence stretch. Finally, he said, "But I am feeling generous. I have decided that, when we are done here, I will put you in the same cell. Mother and daughter, together at last. Won't that be lovely?"

It was probably a sign of just how bad my situation had gotten, but damned if I didn't feel a little uptick in my confidence. If, in some universe, I might've shared a cell with my mother, then anything was possible.

I answered his smile with one of my own. "And here I thought you were going to kill me."

"Kill you? Of course not. Not when you could keep us strong for years to come."

Be imprisoned as a long-term feeder for these creeps or die killing them instead? No contest.

"You mean like she's doing?" I cut another look at the prisoner. It was Sonja, I realized. She was out of it, the neck of her cloak soaked with her own blood—far diminished from when I'd first seen her in the keep, commanding a room of Trainees as she cut the heart from my roommate.

How formidable was Jacob that he could bring down someone as powerful as her?

"Not like Sonja at all," Jacob said dismissively. "She's being questioned. It remains to be seen whether or not she lives through the day." He shrugged. "You should be relieved. It's my understanding she wants you dead. Very, very much so, in fact. You might say I've saved you."

There was a beat of silence. Did he really expect my appreciation? A quick scan of the sheer might in the room told me now was not the time to disobey. "Um, thank you, I guess?"

Jacob gave me a courtly nod and turned his attention back to the door. "Now. Sonja."

When she didn't answer, her captors gave her a shake.

"Sonja," Jacob barked, "look upon me."

She slowly raised her chin, presenting a look of defiance that surprised me. Not as diminished as I'd thought. She'd once commanded Alcántara to deliver me for her sacrificial table, and seeing her now, I had to fight against my gut response to flee, to hide.

"Is this the child you seek?" he demanded.

As her eyes found me, something in her gaze crystallized, those pale blue irises flash-freezing on me. "How—?"

"How did we get her after you so carelessly let her slip through your grasp?" Jacob chuckled and kicked back in his seat. "Your sister, Freya, is loyal to the old ways. She wishes to make peace." With a grand sweep of his hand, he took in all the girls in the room. "This is her offering."

Sonja's attention snapped from me back to Jacob. "Don't trust my sister. This is a trick. She's loyal to no one. Especially not a bunch of old men." She cast a derisive look over the other vampires at the table. "Her ways are much older than the oldest of you."

"Are you saying that deceit runs in your family?"

"I am saying *strength* does." Sonja enunciated each word with slow, cold precision. "Deceit, however, is a lesson, and it's one my sister has studied well."

A low buzz of discussion hummed through the room. I threw my senses wide, studying faces and tics, trying to get a sense of who were allies and who were enemies.

One of the vampires raised his voice above the din. "I believe Sonja is jealous."

"Or angry," another said. He grabbed the lifeless Acari beside him and pulled her chin from side to side. "These children are the fruits of her isle, after all."

"What say you, Sonja?" Jacob asked. "Is it anger, jealousy, or something else which we read on your face? Treachery, perhaps? Is your plan to take down the Synod, and this is why you cannot seem to manage affairs on your own island? Your leaders die, soldiers break faith, weapons go missing..."

I sucked in a breath, which thankfully nobody noticed.

Sonja pulled her shoulders back, and if I hadn't known better, I'd have guessed she was six-feet tall instead of five. "It is betrayal you read on my face, Brother Jacob. Because if you claim this child for your own, it is *you* who betray *me*. It is I who first found Annelise. And then Freya stole the child for her own. It is *Freya* who wishes to take down the Synod."

At these words, several of the vampires shifted in their

seats as though to attack, but Jacob raised a hand to still them. "I am listening, Sonja."

She gestured to me. "She is the only daughter of Birgit, with blood that is pure on both sides, and it is I who first brought you this information—not Freya."

"You thought to keep the child for your own," one of the vampires said. "While Freya gives her freely to us as a gift."

"As an *accident*." Sonja's voice vibrated through the room, resonating through my body. "The stupid child stumbled into Freya's offering, and now my sister thinks to claim the credit. *You* think to take her from me. That, gentlemen, is *betrayal*."

My mind raced. If Jacob handed me off to Sonja, then that was it for everyone I cared about. I'd die in vain, having helped nobody.

"I will consider it," Jacob said finally. "Now leave us."

She looked pissed. "I will not—"

"*Silence*. You will either leave this room in peace, or you will be brought to a cell where you can think more deeply upon your options. Now, I will sample this fabled child myself. One does not rise so high as I have by accepting without question the word of others."

There was a tense beat of silence, then Sonja gave a perfunctory bow of her head.

"Now, gentlemen." Jacob turned from her to address his companions, the composed host once again.

Not me, though. I sat there with a belly full of ice. Sonja was out there, and if I didn't manage to kill Jacob, I'd be fed on, probably passed around, then delivered to her on a silver platter.

Even if I was able to kill Jacob and by some miracle managed to flee this room, I might still have to face her. And you knew your situation sucked when *that* was the bright side.

As these thoughts tumbled through my head, the vampires

began talking among themselves again, swilling from those crazy Medieval-looking goblets and joking...*look at these children...weak...how soft they are.* Soft. *Heh-heh.*

Congratulations went around, a salute to the new Rising. Toasts were made to fallen allies. A protracted moment was spent revering Dagursson. Less time spent on Fournier.

They discussed Sonja—her possible treachery weighed against that of her sister's. How Alcántara wasn't to be trusted, regardless. They mulled over who else could be installed as leader of the Isle of Night. How they'd need to maintain détente with the other islands to keep the balance of power. Who they'd install where to preserve the old order.

If the names they tossed around were any indication, this "world order" didn't make a lot of space for females. These guys were the oldest of old school.

Rescuing my mother had become a quaint notion. Now it was just about staking Jacob, and I'd be lucky if I was able to pull the blade from my boot and make it to his heart before getting skewered myself. It would've helped if I didn't have to go it alone.

I turned my attention to the other Acari, hoping to find a sign of life among their slack faces. I knew I could've trusted them to help—Regina was there, as was Kenzie, and they'd both been my allies on the Isle—but they were all completely out of it.

I was on my own.

In fact, *I* was *their* only hope.

And by the strange hush that was settling over the room, it appeared feeding time had begun.

CHAPTER TWENTY

Each vampire scooped a girl into his arms. Soon, pale, feminine hands and sheets of hair in all colors were splayed atop the table as Acari sprawled lifeless, veins spilling their lifeblood. The room quickly grew silent but for muted moans and the occasional sucking sound.

Beside me, Jacob cleared his throat.

Panic was a vise on my chest. *My turn.*

I swallowed convulsively, then swallowed again. Flexed my ankle. Was it time for the misericordia? Would it ever be a good time?

His thin, wizened lips curled into a smile. "Is there a problem, Annelise?"

There was no way to get to the blade now. He was watching me too closely. It felt like he saw everything. Like he already knew everything.

I needed him to be distracted. Which meant I needed to let him begin to feed.

"No," I managed. "No problem. So...how should we do this?"

The only vampire I'd ever fed was Carden, and my mind went back to the first time. He'd been wrinkly then, too. Would Jacob's skin plump up as Carden's had? No, Jacob was recognizably much older—had been old when he'd been turned. Carden, meanwhile, hadn't looked aged so much as he'd been... desiccated.

Jacob leaned over and wrapped an awkward arm around my shoulders to pull me closer. He ran a finger along the pulse at my neck. "Such power indeed. I can sense it flowing beneath your skin."

A private little chamber in my heart grew cold. Had Carden sensed my power, too? Was that why he'd wanted to bond with me? I'd always thought it was because he'd been attracted to *me*, but what if I'd been wrong all along? What if, all this time, the only thing he'd been attracted to was the purity of my blood?

But no, I told myself, Carden had never used that power. Which meant he hadn't been using *me*.

Even if I were wrong, I needed something good to cling to just now.

Jacob tucked his face into the crook of my neck and inhaled deeply. He held his breath for a moment, then exhaled a creepy little shivery sigh of anticipation. "I can smell it. Pure. Unsullied."

I had to fight the urge to pull away. The puff of his cool breath along my bare skin repulsed me. "Just get on with it," I heard myself say.

Considering my current position, it was probably stupid to be anything less than completely respectful, but I couldn't help it. Doubts about Carden—not to mention my growing horror about what was about to go down here—left me with a tenuous grasp on common sense.

Jacob didn't like my comment—no surprise there—and he pulled back to catch my eye. "Children of this era need to learn their lessons. How to be biddable. Compliant." Long, bony fingers curled into my shoulders. "You will regret you didn't yield more cheerfully. Perhaps if you show yourself to be more dutiful now, you might earn the privilege of remaining at this table."

Biddable, compliant, dutiful, and freaking *cheerful?* As though I were some lowly wench in the Middle Ages praying the big boys might be so benevolent as to toss her some crumbs.

I ducked my chin in a submissive gesture. It was a way to feign obedience, but mostly it hid the look of pure rage I felt burning on my face. Because Jacob was a toad of a man who should've died hundreds of years ago, and as his sharp nails curled into my flesh, I vowed anew—this vampire would die tonight, if I had to trade my own life to make it happen.

"That is more like it," he said, sounding pleased. "Shall we begin?"

With a nod, I stooped into position. I didn't need to feign submissive trembling—I was pretty much scared out of my mind.

I forced myself to keep my eyes open. I would remain aware through this whole thing. He might bite me, but he didn't own me. I would be in control of my mind. My will.

And then he pounced.

Breath whooshed from my body at the assault. When Carden had fed from me that first time, it'd been a quick prick of my skin followed by subtle pressure. Not this, though. This was a *bite*—violent, painful. Ravenous. He'd grabbed me and was holding on tight, sucking with gusto.

Appreciation for Carden surged through me. It'd been so

different with him, from the very start. Maybe I could still save him. I had to try. Which meant getting on with this plan.

I slid my hand from my lap. Bent my knee. Began to reach for my boot. I'd kill this bastard. And then I'd stake as many of these monsters as I could before they brought me down.

But my movement must've jarred him from his reverie because he pulled away. "You *are* powerful. I taste it. And it is intoxicating." Jacob gazed at me as though he were a lover and whispered, "We will be as one, you and I." And then he leaned in. His eyes were on my lips. His mouth was slick with my blood.

Oh shit. Was he going for a kiss? *Oh hell to the no.*

I twitched away, but his hands only grasped me closer.

Then it hit me. *Oh God. No.* The first time Carden had fed, we'd become bonded. He'd fed, and then we'd kissed. It'd been the kiss that bonded us.

"Come to me, Annelise. Let me taste your mouth." Jacob's breath was cool, like the sigh of air from an opened tomb.

My belly spasmed with horror and repulsion, and I gagged, but that only made Jacob hold me tighter.

Oh no no no.

"No kissing," I screeched, sounding like a child. But I didn't care. I would not bond with this thing.

Instead of getting angry, he laughed; the sound was low and possessive. "I see you're not ready yet. I will make you ready." He ducked back down to my neck and went in for more.

My eyes gaped wide open as he sucked harder than before. Gut-panic overwhelmed me. I couldn't let a bond happen. But I was trapped. He was taking too much, too fast, holding me too tight. I couldn't reach my blade. I couldn't even move.

I shoved at him, trying to create the slightest bit of distance between us. But the more I pushed, the harder those nails curled into me, like talons driving into my flesh.

Sometimes, when Carden fed, a fuzzy, dazed feeling would overcome me. It was always slow to dawn, ebbing and flowing, lapping at me like a summer wave, beckoning me deeper. It'd been soothing, like heat rolling through my veins.

But not now. Now, dizziness hit me, smacking me upside the head and propelling my mind into a slow *chuck-chuck-chuck* spin.

I gritted my teeth to fight the wooziness. I refused to pass out. I was too afraid of where I might wake up.

But I couldn't help it, my mind began to recede. I struggled to remember where I was, what I was about.

My blade. I was here to use it. To kill Jacob.

And he was as distracted as he'd ever be. I had to get to the misericordia, no matter what. I couldn't forget why I was demeaning myself like this. It was to save my mother. Help my friends. Be more than what I'd been these past years. To make my life mean something before it was inevitably taken from me.

As though I might actually be enjoying this, I moaned and turned into him. It allowed me a good angle from which I could let my arm slide from my chair. I strained to reach my boot, but it was no good. He still held me too tightly.

I made another small sound in my throat and angled more, pressing my body into him. He didn't fight me this time. I was able to shift a little, and the movement made his teeth tug at my neck, tearing my skin.

I pretended my pain didn't exist. That was one valuable trick the vampires had taught me.

My fingers splayed, reaching. They brushed the top of my boot. I needed to snag it before I blacked out. Surely he'd slow down soon, maybe pull back enough for me to reach.

But Jacob wasn't stopping, and a dark fog began to spread over my mind. As the blood left my body, warmth went with it.

My brain felt cool. My hands and feet prickled with cold, then my limbs. I flexed my feet, hoping desperately to work some blood back into my extremities.

Panic spiraled through me. I needed to maintain control. Stay aware. I needed to get this done—now.

Jacob finally pulled away, whispering, "Now are you ready?"

He wanted that kiss. And I wanted my blade. Let's see who wanted what more.

"Sure," I managed to say.

Jacob was kissing his way up my neck to my jaw, and something about his zeal suddenly struck me as absurd. It cleared my head. I coughed to buy myself a second's more time.

It was like I'd broken a trance, because then another cough came from across the table, and it gave me pause. Someone coughing wasn't so strange—the girls had been making tiny noises, coughing and whimpering, since this feeding had begun. But there'd been something odd about this cough.

This one had come from a male throat.

It happened again, and I froze, trying to interpret the unexpectedness of it. I was on alert now, my senses flung out to the room.

Then another vampire cleared his throat, coming from my left this time. But this time, Jacob froze, too, his eyes dancing around the table in confusion.

Vampires were pulling away from their victims. They'd all begun to cough. Then to gag and retch.

As though a light was switched, all the girls' eyes snapped to life. Bright, female gazes swept the room.

They were awake. I wasn't alone.

Clara, the older Watcher, caught my eye. She cocked a brow, looking like some sort of wicked pirate queen.

My body fizzed to life, giddy with possibility. My hand went to my boot, to my blade. I wasn't alone, and we would take these bastards down.

Game on.

Kenzie shouted, "Now."

CHAPTER TWENTY-ONE

I was amazed, which meant I was distracted. I didn't see the hand that swung out to grab my throat.

The other vampires looked poisoned, but not Jacob. He looked pissed.

"Is this *your* trick?" His fingers dug in, and I felt the tiny bones of my throat bend. He was crushing my windpipe.

My feet scrambled beneath my chair, trying to get purchase, but I couldn't propel myself to standing. I couldn't get away.

I was weak from blood loss. It was making me act stupid. Because instinctively, I began to claw at his hands. But in my mind, I knew: in this case, instinct was wrong. There was no pulling away from a pair of strong hands determined to choke the life from me.

Dimly from behind me, I heard a clatter. Several female voices cheering. I wasn't alone, I reminded myself. Every Acari in this room was fighting, and it was my turn.

I stopped struggling. Stopped trying to breathe, even. I refused to let panic kill me. My rational mind clicked to life.

I let go of Jacob's arms. I'd lasted longer than this without breath, and so for this moment, I would let him try to strangle me. I bent my knee instead, trying to grab hold of my heel, but it slipped from my hand.

Black spots began to blip in my vision, and I forced my heart to slow. I had no use for adrenaline right now. *Calm*, I repeated in my head. *Be calm.*

I tried again, kicking my heel back hard. This time, I managed to grab hold. My fingers grazed the hilt. Got purchase. I slid the misericordia from my boot, and a different sort of adrenaline burst through my veins. It was exhilaration.

I would've sworn the blade hummed as it hit the air. The metal was warm, nestling in my palm with a pulse of power.

Jacob had gone to the edge of his chair, angled toward me, his complete focus on me. He thought he was choking me.

I met his eyes, held them. There was a flicker of confusion in his as he saw the smile curl my lips.

I swung my arm up and around, and I brought the blade toward us, slamming it into his back. His eyes went wide as he collapsed into me.

I'd missed his heart, but it was okay. I was only getting started.

I pulled out the misericordia and shoved him away. Rage thrummed through me until I was electric with it, lit from within as I flew to my feet. I stood over him and swung the blade in a shimmering arc. It sang as it cut through the air.

Time froze as I saw the moment he realized which blade I wielded. Just as he'd pounced on me before, I pounced on him. Heaving all my weight behind the misericordia, I thrust it into his heart. I roared as I struck, wishing I could kill him a thousand times.

Like oil hitting a scalding hot skillet, blood spattered up at me, his flesh smoking and sizzling. Jacob's mouth yawned wide, and the sound that erupted from him was inhuman, an ear-piercing squeal, both bellowing and shrill. Now *he* was the one clawing at *my* wrists, but I held the blade firm.

"Like it?" my injured throat was hoarse, but still I managed to mimic that same creepy, loverly tone of voice he'd used earlier. "You said you wanted to get closer." His body sizzled as the handle of the blade grew scalding hot. But I held fast, twisting until smoke billowed from his wound. "This is how girls of 'my era' do things."

His body bucked and shuddered, and I hopped back, avoiding him as he toppled from the chair, hitting the ground.

Dead.

I stood there for a second, panting, heart thudding. My vision was still warped and dimmed around the edges. I'd lost a lot of blood. Probably the only reason I was still standing was the months I'd spent bonded to Carden.

Grunting and the wet sound of impaled flesh made me tune into the violence that had erupted around me. I looked to see where I could help, but the fight between Acari and Vampire was already slowing.

The vampires had been impaired by their feeding, but they were a tenacious bunch, and it took several strikes to fell a single one. But the reanimated girls were fierce and magnificent, and they'd triumphed.

Bye-bye, old world order.

It struck me what a ragtag bunch this was, young Acari battling alongside older Guidons and one Watcher.

Life on the Isle of Night was all conflict and rivalry. So how had a bunch of random Acari organized and masterminded this? More than merely disabling the vampires, these girls had arrived armed with hidden weapons. The moment a stake was lost, another would appear in hand.

A dreadful feeling took root in the back of my mind. An unthinkable thought.

I watched the fighting as though through the ponderous click of a camera shutter. When someone lost a weapon, she'd just pop an elbow to release a carved wooden stake hidden up her sleeve.

Crude stakes hidden along forearms—it was signature Ronan.

Was he a part of this? Had *he* been the force to unite this ragtag warrior crew?

I looked around, and my eyes landed on Regina. Grinning broadly, she gave me a little wave, and it was all so surreal. Because despite the fact that I needed to be thinking about Sonja, about my mother, a single thought had barreled to the forefront of my mind. It'd taken hold and wouldn't let go.

Ronan.

Was I right? Was he behind this? Had I wrongly doubted him, then sent him to an uncertain fate?

A hand grasped my ankle. I staggered but kept my footing.

A vampire was still alive at my feet.

"Bastard." I kicked at him. "I am so done with all of you."

I dropped to my knees, misericordia poised in my hand. I was all too happy to have a chance to use it again. It was bastards like this who'd taken my mother from me in the first place. Who'd made me doubt Ronan.

The vampire grew still as he saw what I held. "Ah. So it is." He lifted his chin proudly. Ropes of blood and spittle ran down his fangs as he said, "You can't kill us all." He shut his eyes on a deep exhale.

And I staked him.

You can't kill us all. He was right. I'd never get to all the bad guys in the world. It was impossible to eradicate every evil, to kill every vampire.

But I didn't need to. All that was left was Sonja. The rest could kiss my ass and wave goodbye when I made my way off this island.

But for now, Sonja was still out there. My mother was still in a cell.

And Ronan. Always, Ronan.

I wasn't done here, not nearly.

I wobbled to standing, jittery and shaking from all the adrenaline rushes. I blinked hard, realizing my vision was swimming. Tears had blurred my eyes, and I wiped a rough arm across my face.

I looked to Kenzie and managed to ask, "You guys were faking it? You weren't really unconscious?"

"Some of us were injured badly enough, but yeah." Her nod was sharp and proud. "Ronan set it up."

"Ronan." My voice cracked on his name.

"He insisted on coming." Watcher Clara popped her knuckles. "I was just psyched to get a shot at taking these sleazebags down. But he said you needed him. I guess you've got a mom here or something?"

The new girl was shaking her head. "Dude, that is so fucked up."

I wanted to laugh. It was such a preposterous, astounding plan—only Ronan could've come up with it. And then I wanted to cry. He hadn't betrayed me. I was the one who'd betrayed him.

"We drank feverfew tea," Regina added. "It's like poison for vampires."

"Not poison," Kenzie corrected. "Blood thinner. Feverfew oil is a natural element—"

"Comes from a daisy," another Acari interjected.

Kenzie nodded. "It's used in natural medicine to prevent coagulation. Minimal side effects for humans."

"But catastrophic for vampires," Regina added with enthusiasm. "It incapacitates them when they drink it."

"Temporarily," Kenzie corrected her. "Just long enough to stake them."

Regina turned to me, her grin even broader, if that was possible. "He's a genius."

"Who?" I barely got the word out, my throat was so tight. But I knew before she said it.

"Ronan." She gave me a playful nudge, as if to say *duh*.

Duh. Ronan. Forever Ronan. Duh duh duh.

"Genius?" an older girl said. She wore the uniform of a Guidon, and her navy-blue catsuit was shining, soaked with blood. "He's a *hottie*."

"Watch it." Kenzie flicked her eyes to me. "I think he's taken." Then she winked at me.

Winked.

I thought I might vomit.

Regina had probably long suspected the true depth of my feelings for him, because now she was chattering blithely on, clueless as to how her words were slaying me. "Coming over here," she relayed gleefully, "Ronan was all, *when we get to Annelise*-this and *Annelise will know what to do*-that."

"All in that accent," the Guidon sighed. *"Annelise will understand what I'm about,"* she mimicked, then rolled her eyes in mock ecstasy.

But I didn't understand, did I? I hadn't trusted him.

In my mind, I pictured those green eyes in the rearview mirror. How they'd locked with mine.

Haunted. In pain.

I knew what that pain might've felt like. I'd thought he was betraying me, but all along, I'd been the treacherous one. So quick to doubt him.

I'd been the one to cause his pain. It was agony.

He cared for me. But I hadn't trusted it. I hadn't *seen*.

He'd tried to communicate his plan, but I'd blown him off. *Oh, God*, worse, I said I could never love someone like him.

Even stupid Charlotte had seen. She'd seen his love and taken him away.

I'd been the one to double-cross him. And it was most likely getting him killed right now.

Well, I was damned if I'd let that happen. Finally, Ronan's true feelings for me had penetrated my thick skull. Finally, my scarred little heart was beating with the knowledge that maybe he loved me.

That *I* definitely loved *him*.

What did that mean about my feelings for Carden? I adored being with my vampire. He was so easy.

Too easy.

Carden was all about greasing the wheels, making people happy, and getting as close as he could to his goals. Carden had been prioritizing his mission over me since we'd met. His goals were honorable, sure. But they weren't *my* goals.

And then there was Ronan. *We* had the same goals. Valued the same things. We'd fight for what we believed in, even if it meant our own downfall. We treasured friends, helped allies, longed for family, and all along, held the fierce desire to keep a portion of ourselves private, separated from what we saw as a world of horrors.

It was Ronan who made me want to be a better person. Ronan, like me, was never willing to compromise. We never greased wheels. It was Ronan who'd save a girl from cafeteria bullies while Carden chose to sit idly by.

Both men were good and noble, but it was Ronan who'd sacrifice his own happiness, his own life, to ensure the safety of those he cared about.

And that sounded a lot like me. Like who I was, who I wanted to be.

Vampire, Tracer, Watcher, it didn't matter. Ronan and I were as bonded as two could be. Being parted from him like this was pain worse than any blood fever.

My body felt light, expansive. I was full of air, like I might float from the ground.

I was in love with him.

How had I not known all this time? It was obvious. Inevitable. From the moment I first saw him in that stupid university office in Florida, my feelings had been as fixed and fated as my need for air, for sustenance. No less than those things, Ronan was a part of me. I needed him in my life.

I needed to find him.

The memory of what I'd done and said pierced the balloon in my chest. Would he forgive me? His sister had sworn to destroy me. Would he side with her?

Resolution seemed impossible.

But I wouldn't think about that. A fire had been lit inside me, and I truly believed that once Ronan and I were together, we could figure anything out.

Whatever happened with my mother, Ronan was just as much my family. I chose him. We were kindred. Because, as I've learned, my mother could turn out to be anyone. Bloodlines don't mean anything. Look at Lilac as proof of that.

It was time to act. I looked at the girls around me. They were my family, too. We were in this together. My power, their power—it was *our* power.

I pulled my shoulders back and held that misericordia aloft like a torch. "We have to find Ronan."

I guess I'd snarled the words, because my earnestness made a couple of the older girls laugh.

"Chill," Clara said. "Of course we'll find him. I saw exactly where they took him."

Kenzie smiled. "Then let's go save the guy."

CHAPTER TWENTY-TWO

The new Acari caught up with Clara and clapped her on the shoulder. "Girl, you're short, but you are fast." If I hadn't already known she was a brand-new recruit, speaking to a Watcher with such clueless irreverence would've been a quick indication.

But Clara wasn't mad when she turned and jogged backward to face us. She was fierce, and with her solid gait and brown hair spilling all over the place, she looked like an action hero, like someone who'd face off with a cyborg killing machine using just her wits and a stick. "I'm not short." She grinned. "I'm fun-sized."

Clara, Regina, and me were like the petite brigade. I'd hated my height for years, but now, no way. I'd come to understand just how awesome "fun-sized" was. Just then, it felt like we could sneak into anywhere, make our way through anything.

Kenzie slowed her pace. "Not so fast, ladies. We need a weapons check." She led us into a dim alcove off the main hallway. "Show me what you got."

"Good call." I sidled in beside her. "Does everyone have something?"

We were whispering, even though the entire floor seemed abandoned. My guess was, once those Synod dudes were in a meeting, everyone else held all their calls.

"I've only got one stake left," Regina said, "but I do have this." And then she slipped a thin, beltlike cord from around her waist.

One of the Guidons peered closer. "Bloody hell. Is that a garrote?"

Hearing the British accent placed her identity for me. "Juliet, right?"

She gave me a nod and a smile. "Hiya, D." Then she hefted a fireplace poker in the air. "I nicked this from the hearth."

"Score." The other Guidon, a girl named Mala, looked impressed. Then her face fell as she rubbed her forearm. "All I've got is two stakes. I'll make it work, though."

"You couldn't sneak your weapon from the Isle?" I asked, because it sure seemed like these girls had managed to smuggle in a veritable armory tucked away in sleeves, pants, and boots.

"The weapon they assigned me? It's a pike." Mala raised her brows in disdain. "Yeah. Hate that thing. It's a miracle I'm still alive."

Clara lifted her hands like a surgeon who'd just scrubbed. "This is all I need."

"Bollocks," Juliet said. "You're going to face these guys with your bare hands?"

"All right, all right." Clara bent and pulled a pair of nunchucks from her boots. "Meet Chuckie."

I couldn't fight the laugh that burst from me. "I've always wanted to try those."

"Shush." Kenzie put up a hand to quiet me. She nodded her chin at the new girl. "Whatcha got?"

"My stakes are gone." The poor kid seemed stricken. She probably had barely any experience fighting her newbie peers, much less facing a coven of ancient, pissed off vampires. "I had a switchblade, but lost it in the fight."

"Don't sweat it." Kenzie pulled two stakes from her sleeves and handed them to her. "Use these."

"What's your name?" I asked her.

"Monique."

"Monique, you can stick by me," I told her and attempted a reassuring smile. I was liking this whole girl bonding thing. I turned to Kenzie. "If she's got your stakes, what will you use?"

Kenzie pulled up her shirt, wriggled a bit, then slid a sai knife from each hip. They looked a little like tridents and a lot like something a manga badass might wield. She grinned. "Didn't manage to give these an airing before the last fight was over. How about you?" She pointed to my misericordia. "Where'd you get that little slice of awesome?"

"Yeah," Mala said. "What the hell is that thing?"

"Misericordia." I held it up, but didn't pass it around. "The vampires use it to kill...well...to kill us; it's a quickie way to make more vampires. But it also kills *them*. Every time." I bent to run a hand along the side of my boot, checking to make sure my shuriken and my awesome new boomerang were still safely tucked away. "I've got my throwing stars, too. But they won't do much good against these guys."

"So shall we?" An evil smile curved a corner of Clara's lips. "Not that I'm not enjoying this little tea party, but I'm kinda jonesing to kick some vampire ass."

I gave her a fist bump. I liked this girl's attitude. "Just tell us where they're hiding Ronan."

"Two floors up." She gave me a look that was part trepidation, part apology. "He's with his sister."

"Guards?"

"Is the pope Catholic?"

"Guards and stuff," Monique said. "Can we handle all that?"

"Sure we can," Kenzie said.

"And we will." I squeezed Monique's shoulder. "Don't freak out. We got this. Stick by me."

We made our way to the elevator, and Clara held out an arm to stop us. "This floor is quiet, but the rest of this place is a freaking hive. So heads up."

I eyed the elevator. It was the artery that connected the whole factory. But we needed to act fast. Anyone could emerge from it at any second. I pressed the button.

Juliet frowned. "Is that wise?"

"Gotta get up there somehow." I told her, "You, Kenzie, Mala, and Monique will ride in the elevator."

Monique took a step back. "Isn't there, like, a sneaky back stairwell or something?"

"What are *we* going to do?" Clara looked disappointed that she might miss the fight. "Shouldn't we stick together?"

"Totally." I beamed. I was a part of something. I'd always wanted a family, and here I'd found sisters in the most unexpected of places. "We fun-sized girls will be riding *on top* of the elevator."

Regina's eyes widened. "On top?"

"Oh yeah." Clara high-fived me. "Always wanted to do that."

"On top," Regina repeated flatly.

Mala gave her a little shove. "Did you not see *any* of the Die Hard movies?"

We were out of time. The elevator dinged. Monique held

the door as the other three helped us reach up, slide the ceiling panel aside, and climb on top of the car.

We got the panel back in place, plunging us into shadows. The only light came from the car below us, filtered up through an old-fashioned wrought-iron screen. Otherwise, the floor— their roof—was surprisingly smooth, bisected only by a giant steel bar that connected us to the top of the factory high above. There were wheels like pulleys connected to three thick cables.

"That doesn't seem like a lot to hold us," Regina whispered.

Clara hissed. "How do you know what an elevator roof is supposed to look like?"

I put a finger to my lips to shush them.

There was a mechanical *whoosh* and a chime. Then the thing began to move.

We'd started five floors underground.

All we needed to do was go up two floors.

We stopped after one.

I met Regina's eyes. They looked like they were about to bulge from their sockets.

There was a cheerful little *ding*.

Our heads knocked together as we all knelt to peer through the metal scrollwork panel. All I could see were the tops of the other girls' heads—blond, black, black, brown. Their stances were taut, feet braced apart, hands on weapons.

The door slid open.

Three vampires stood there. Slow smiles spread across their faces as they shared a look.

I held my breath, and Regina pinched my arm.

One of the vampires chuckled. "Well, well."

The door began to slide shut. A robed arm shot out to stop it.

The vampires edged inside.

CHAPTER TWENTY-THREE

The doors whooshed shut, and we began to move again. One of the vampires—a tall, gaunt creature with a gray face and thin reddish hair that told me he wasn't so old when he'd been turned—reached out and traced a line down Kenzie's cheek. "What a pleasant surprise."

"Here we go," Clara said under her breath.

I whispered, "Wait for it."

The other two vampires were no different, eyeing the girls as though they'd won that evening's grand surprise buffet.

A short, balding one turned to Juliet and asked in a voice meant to be charming, "Shall we get acquainted with these lovelies?"

"Let's do." The tall guy raised his hand to the *stop* button.

Mala didn't hesitate. Before he could reach it, she staked his palm to the panel's wooden frame.

And like a bomb being detonated, the elevator exploded into madness.

The tall vampire's eyes rolled with fury as he worked to

pull his hand free, but before he could, Mala slid her other stake into her hand and drove it through his chest.

She hit the button then, and the car shuddered to an abrupt stop, and we had to hold onto each other and that huge steel crossbar to steady ourselves on top.

I slid the panel aside. One vamp down, two to go. The fight had already begun, and I wasn't about to miss it.

"I know you guys wanted to go up," I said as swung my legs over the side. I leapt down, misericordia already in my hand, and fell onto the short vampire, driving the blade into his chest as I landed. "But you're going down instead."

By the time I stood up, the third vampire had already been dispatched, and Kenzie was wiping her sai knives clean with the edge of a monk's cloak. "Really, D? *Going down?* You went there?"

"Sorry." I gave them a rueful smile. "I joke when I'm nervous."

We needed to keep plowing ahead while we still had the nerve. While Ronan was still alive.

I poised my finger to disengage the *stop* button. "Everyone ready?"

Everyone nodded.

"As I'll ever be," Monique said.

The elevator moved again and in seconds we were at the third floor. Kenzie held the *open* button as we adjusted to the sight revealed before us.

The doors had opened onto a sumptuous hallway, moodily lit. A rich, amber glow emanated from wrought-iron sconces along the wall, shimmering along burgundy velvet wallpaper and smoked mirror panels that lined the hall.

"Posh," Juliet whispered beside me.

Regina whispered, "What is this, the Playboy Mansion?"

I heard footsteps. A distant door shutting. The bored murmurs of guards.

Soon they'd wonder who was in the elevator and why they weren't getting out.

I had the misericordia in my hand and my friends by my side. "Now or never," I said and stepped out.

About a dozen vampires were guarding the hall. It took only half a beat of confusion on their part before they leapt at us.

Like some sick, brutal dance, we broke into pairs. My partner was a snarling vamp in a green uniform who was running straight for me. I set my stance and faced him full-on.

He leapt. I grabbed his throat as we fell backward. But he was too close for me to get my blade into position. As we toppled, my mind went into training mode. I let myself drop to my butt, smoothly rolling back the moment I hit the floor. I kept rolling. Hitched up my knees. Flipped him right over me.

Where Juliet was waiting. She impaled him with her fireplace poker the moment he landed. "Brilliant," she shouted. "I love this thing."

"Thanks for the save," I called up at her, but she'd already turned and was fighting two-on-three with Regina by her side.

I heard Regina gasp, and I spared her a quick glance. She'd been sliced down the side.

But then the vampires around her gasped, too.

The vampire who'd slashed her recoiled. Turned his back to her to recover. "What is that stench?"

The feverfew oil must still be coursing through the girls' veins.

"I think the phrase you're looking for is *Trojan horse*." I sprang to my feet. "Unnerving, isn't it? Almost as unnerving as being taken from our homes by a bunch of bloodsucking assholes."

As I spoke, I spotted the reflection of another vamp sneaking up behind me. I had no problems gripping my blade this time. In a single, fluid move, I whirled around and staked him.

"Hey, vampires do have reflections," I shouted to no one in particular.

Regina came to stand back-to-back with me, and we did a slow turn, ready for the next attack. "These mirrors are freaking me out," she said.

"I like them," Watcher Clara called out enthusiastically.

I sought her in the melee and found her gripping a shard of mirror in her hand, standing over a vamp body riddled with more mirror fragments.

"You're intense," I said.

She gave me a little salute. "I could say the same."

A female gasp got my attention, and my eyes found Monique. I'd told her to stay close, but this fight was too chaotic, and I'd lost her. Now a vampire had her by the throat and he was sliding her up the side of the wall.

"Don't you dare." I bounded toward them, throwing two stars as I ran, but they pinged off of his back, doing no good.

Before I could reach her, a stake appeared in her hand. She used one hand to strike the vampire's elbow, and when his arm buckled, she swung her other arm down and skewered him in the throat. She landed on her feet with a growl. "You messed with the wrong girl."

Kenzie shouted, "Go Monique!"

The new Acari was rubbing her throat and panting to catch her breath. "I learned from the best," she rasped with a half-smile.

That smile was cut short when a bearded vamp grabbed her from behind. His fingers curled into her upper arms until blood bloomed like dark roses along her sleeves.

He peered at the blood, sniffing deeply. His mouth twisted in repulsion. "What deceit is this?"

Clara launched herself onto his back. "You're the ones who have trouble with impulse control." She gritted out the words as she got a hold of his chin with one hand and cupped the top of his head with her other. With a sharp twist to her arms, she propelled herself backward. The crack of his neck reverberated around us.

The instant he dropped to the ground, a few of us were on him, staking him before he could rise again.

Clara looked indignant. "I was getting to that."

Mala shrugged. "I was feeling left out."

Talk about fun-sized—I looked around, feeling about ten feet tall. We'd thinned the guards considerably. And though we'd all sustained injuries, for the vampires, it seemed to have backfired. The scent of the girls' blood was in the air now and it was disturbing them. Throwing them off balance.

One older vampire was hanging back, watching as his fellows were being systematically downed. He struck me as the type to scurry into a hole when times got tough. I didn't want him to get away and alert anyone.

"A survivor." I strolled toward him, then enjoyed making a mocking curtsey. "Care to dance?"

He didn't like that. His lips peeled back in a hiss.

"Tut-tut." I raised my misericordia with a smile, and it had the same immediate, dramatic effect it'd had on the other vamps. I shook my head in amazement. "This will never get old."

He summoned something inside himself and pulled to his full height. He must've used some kind of vampire mojo, because he seemed to expand to an unnatural size and his voice took on a deep, resounding vibrato. "You know not whom you face." And then he stalked toward me, like he might overcome me.

"You don't scare me," I murmured. And then I broke into a run. Straight for him.

Taken aback, he was suddenly normal height again. Or maybe it was just my perception. Maybe I could see through their tricks now.

He hadn't changed. *I had.*

I staked him, and the spot where my blade struck burst into a low, smoldering flame.

I turned. We were done. We'd gotten them all.

I grinned at each girl in turn, appreciating every single one of them. "Well—"

The next thing I knew, Regina was flying past me, garrote in hand.

I turned in time to see her clothesline the vamp I'd just killed, catching him at the neck. He fell, throat slashed halfway through.

We watched as his burning body shuddered back to standing.

"Again?" I stared at the red and black smoking fissure where his ribcage should've been. I'd missed his heart the first time, and now he was shambling toward me, swinging his arms erratically, trying to grab me.

"What the fuck?" Clara scowled. "How old is this guy?"

Regina shouted, "Finish him, D."

"My pleasure." I dodged and staked him again, making sure not to miss his heart this time.

Regina began to squeal, putting me back on instant alert. Tiny orange embers had caught the ends of her curly hair.

I dashed to her side to pat them out. "I burned my hair once," I told her. "I don't recommend it."

She thanked me, but I was quick to say, "Thank *you*. That was a nice save."

Kenzie came over, hands on hips, those sai knives still clutched tightly in her fists. "I think this fight is over."

"Looks like they were guarding that." I pointed to a door at the end of the hallway.

Ronan. Hold on. I'm almost there.

"Let's think this through," Juliet said.

But I was done thinking. By the time she finished speaking, I was already running toward it. Toward him.

Until a figure popped from the shadows in front of me. I staggered to a halt with a shout, genuinely startled, torn from my laser-focus.

"Boo." It was Sonja, and she was laughing. "You're so predictable, chasing after your boys as you do. Run, run, Annelise, like a child mad for a toy. But I've caught you. Charlotte led you right to me. And now I will have your strength. *My beautiful boys* will have your strength." She chucked me on the chin, and I flinched away.

I held my right hand at my thigh, the misericordia tucked along my forearm, out of her sight. She still didn't know I had her blade.

I made like I was considering her words. "Yeahhh...nope. I'm not in a sharing mood, Sonja. Now get out of my way."

This was the vampire who'd controlled the Isle of Night from the shadows. Who'd masterminded the death of so many of my friends. Who'd betrayed her own sex in search of more and more power.

It had been *Sonja's* circus of violence and brutality that'd taught me how to fight. That had trained me not to tip my hand. Now I'd make Sonja suffer the lesson she'd taught me. I'd keep my weapon—the weapon I'd stolen from her—hidden until the last possible second.

That was some delicious irony right there.

A coquettish grin shone from her face. "Tell me, did you come for Ronan? Or is Carden still the flavor of the month?"

I widened my eyes in mock surprise. "I think you just insulted me."

Her face shriveled into a sneer. "You think they care about you, but it's me they—"

I was shaking my head. "I'm going to stop you right there. I'm done playing your sick game."

Done with people hurting me.

Done losing friends, being estranged from family.

Done with Sonja's cruel, narcissistic rule of *Eyja næturinnar*.

My arm flashed up, and the misericordia was an arrow aimed for her heart.

I staked her. Hard.

"Now to answer your question." I staked her again for good measure, and again, even after she lay smoldering on the ground. "I came here for *all* the people I care about."

I pulled the blade free one final time with a crackle of smoke and sputtering blood.

"I think you got her," Kenzie said, sounding amused.

We all stood there in silence staring down at the body. Had I really just killed Sonja?

"That was quick," Clara said, and then she began to laugh. "I expected... I don't know..."

Monique looked at her in amazement. "What, you wanted *more* drama?"

"A quick kill? I'll take it." I slung an arm around Mala and one around Regina, but my eyes were glued to the door at the end of the hall. "And now it's time for door number three."

CHAPTER TWENTY-FOUR

The elevator dinged.

We shared exasperated glances at the hushed sound of the doors sliding open. "No freaking way," Mala groaned. "More of them?"

I looked from the elevator to the doorway and back again.

Kenzie put her hand on my shoulder. "We got this. You go find Ronan."

"Watch out for Charlotte," Clara added. "I knew her before she 'died' the first time. She was a pain in my ass. Go kill her for real now."

I nodded, but the idea didn't sit well. Could I kill Ronan's only sister? What if it came down to her or me—whom would he choose? The thought was unsettling.

Male shouting echoed from down the hall. The vampires had found the carnage.

"Everyone knows we're here now." Juliet gave me a shove. "Go. We'll see you on the outside."

"But..." I looked from girl to girl. Would they be able to find their way back to the surface? I thought of all the vampires they'd face between here and the mainland. "Don't you need all the help you can get?"

Clara gave me an exaggeratedly disparaging scowl. "I think we can survive without your help, little D."

Finally, I nodded. "Okay, but that's Fun-Sized D to you."

A couple of the girls gave me extra shoves as I spun and went for the door. A cacophony of clashing and snarling exploded behind my back.

I tuned it out.

I had a very different fight ahead of me.

I didn't give myself a moment to think. My hand was on the old-fashioned glass doorknob. I turned it. Stepped inside.

My eyes found Ronan at once. I couldn't look away. He was seated on a lush, upholstered chair. He wasn't tied, but something held him in place. Pain? Hidden bonds? Vampire mojo?

"Ronan?" my voice cracked on his name.

Slowly his head turned to me. Dread churned in my belly, and it gave my body a sick, swampy feeling, because what would be in his eyes when he saw me? Anger...hatred...disappointment...I don't know which would be the worst.

He saw me. His eyes blinked hard. Was it tears? Disbelief? Or had Charlotte simply beat the crap out of him?

He looked confused.

My heart fell. Had I destroyed the trust we'd built together with one massively stupid mistake?

I deflated even more. Because it wasn't just a single, stupid mistake on my part. I'd been doing stupid stuff since I'd arrived on the Isle of Night.

But then his gaze seemed to focus, and that Ronan light I knew and loved so well kindled to life in his forest-green eyes. He was ablaze in there, in his heart. I saw it. And it was aimed at me. "Ann?" he rasped.

There was a supernova in my chest—relief, excitement,

giddiness, heat—all the feelings, so many of them new, unfurled in me. I ran to him.

"Your mother. Did you find her?" He tried to rise, but staggered and fell back into his seat.

"Oh my God, oh my God, it's okay, Ronan. Sit down." I fell to my knees before him, searching his body for injury. "Are you all right? I didn't find my mom yet, but I just...I needed to find you first. I *had* to see you. We'll get you out of here. But, oh God, you must hate me. I'm so sorry. Will you forgive me? Can you ever forgive me? I don't know why I didn't trust you. You just, I don't know, it's your *sister*. You always talked—"

"Shush, Ann. Get up here." His hands were reaching for me.

I propelled myself into his arms. My body nestled onto his lap like a puzzle piece finding its place.

I pulled away to look at him, and my heart skipped in my chest. I felt insubstantial. As though it were only his arms around me that held me grounded to the earth.

The eyes that met mine smoldered, but it was his hands that set me alight. Smoothing over my body. Down my back and along my thighs. Through my hair. All the while murmuring, "I'm fine, but your neck. What happened? Are you okay? Are you hurt? Did they hurt you?"

"I'm fine. It's nothing. That doesn't matter. But, oh Ronan..." My eyes held his as I waited for my throat to unclench. "Ronan, I am so sorry."

"It's okay, love. It's—"

He'd called me *love*. I was undone.

I cut him off with a fierce hug, wrapping my arms around his neck, tangling my fingers in his hair.

Breathing him in.

He laughed low and quiet, giving me a squeeze, then easing back. He held my face in his hands, our noses mere inches apart. He whispered, "Don't punish yourself. This is a terrifying, confusing place. I understand. I dared not tell you the plan in front of Carden, but I knew you'd get it eventually. I have faith in you, Ann. I always do. From the first moment we sat together in that ridiculous car, I had faith."

I couldn't speak, overcome with emotion.

So I kissed him instead.

I was out of words, but apparently my body had no trouble expressing itself. It was a riot of feeling. My shoulders loosened, releasing all the tension of being apart, while other, more secret parts of me tightened until I felt I couldn't get enough of him.

I would never be satisfied. I could never get close enough.

We broke the kiss on a gasp.

He rested his forehead on mine. "Actually, maybe I don't forgive you. I might enjoy having you make it up to me."

Ronan saying naughty things.

My body sizzled.

"Yeah," I managed to breathe, "I think we can work something out."

He leaned in to kiss me again, slowly this time. Carefully. Like he was memorizing me for a test.

"Annelise." His eyes met mine, and the fire in his gaze had eased into something warm. Enduring. "I love you, you know."

The words washed over me, a soothing, cleansing wave. "Oh, Ronan. I love you, too. I think I always have. It's something that's always been there. Like, I don't know, it's like air. You don't think about air. How you need it? But I need you, Ronan. You're my air. My heart. I'd be lost without you. I don't want to be without you."

His expression froze. I had a moment's panic that I'd said too much, but then his eyes flicked to the side.

I knew that look.

I went into Acari mode. Someone was at my back. In half a

second, I'd assessed the location of my every weapon and how far they were from my hands. I began to reach.

Too late.

Charlotte had me by my neck. "*Brava*, young Annelise. You found us. I didn't think you'd make it. My brother said I underestimated you. He said too much, actually." She dragged me off his lap. "I believe you're becoming a bit of a distraction for young Ronan. And I don't like distractions."

She flung me to the floor.

"Lottie. Enough." Ronan was on his feet, but I saw how he had to lock his knees to stay upright.

I scrambled away from her and hopped up. "What did you do to him?"

I felt the misericordia in my boot, but I didn't want to bring it out yet. I still had hope this family might resolve things. It seemed preposterous, but what other choice did I have? I couldn't slaughter Ronan's sister in front of him.

"I had to drug him. It seemed somehow fitting, considering his little trick earlier." Charlotte strolled over to scruff Ronan's hair. "That's why he's so weak." She leaned close to his ear. "You're weak, Ro. You have such potential power within your reach, and you don't take it. You think you need people, but you don't."

"I need her," he said, his eyes not budging from me. "I need Annelise."

She shoved his head. "Pathetic."

But he stayed standing. "There is no cause for you to behave like this, Lottie. We share too much. We share a family. A history. Can you not let me go to be my own man?"

"Let you go?" She repeated the words, infusing them with a mix of outrage and disdain. "Let you go? What do you think this place is? A resort you can stroll away from any time you wish? Who do you think you are? You have power. You must use it. Or someone will come along and use it for you." A smile peeled across her face. "Just like we're using her mommy. Her mommy had power and didn't want to use it. And look what happened."

She wandered to me and petted her hand over my head. And then again harder, then harder still. "Your mommy was asking after you. Such a shame you need to watch her die. Shall we go to her now?"

I slapped her hand away. I was ready for a fight. "Your days of using my mother are done. I'm not leaving without her."

"Then it looks like you're not leaving. Because there are a lot of vampires who would give much to have you infuse their bloodline."

Ronan stepped forward. "You won't harm her. And you won't harm her mother, either."

I felt it then. Ronan's power, so familiar to me now, rippled through the room.

Charlotte staggered. Caught herself. She turned on him with a snarl. "You think to use your power on me? We might've been born with the same blood running through our veins, but I'm a vampire now, Ronan. Think twice before you cross me."

I pulled my shoulders back and stepped between them to face her. "I, on the other hand, have no trouble crossing you. So leave him out of this."

She laughed. "You're not strong enough to face me, little girl. You're barely tall enough."

Insulting my height, now that was beyond the pale. It was time.

"Yeah," I said as I pulled out the misericordia, "but this might help."

A random thought blipped in the back of my mind: where was Carden? Shouldn't he pop in at any second? It was his way to swoop in at the last second. To make his grand entrance and save me with a wink and a jest.

Charlotte flicked a cursory glance over my blade, and for a moment, I thought maybe she didn't recognize what it was. But when her eyes met mine again, hers had hardened. "You're a clever brat. No matter. My brother won't let me die." She turned her head to look at him. "Will you, Ro?"

Ronan's voice softened. "Of course I don't want you to die, Charlotte. I would never want that. Remember when we were children? Chasing crabs by the shore, racing the waves? That girl is still inside you. Remember her. Remember yourself. You're a part of me, Lottie." His arm slid around my shoulders, warm and firm. "But if you try to harm Annelise, there will be consequences."

Her eyes narrowed. "So does this mean you've chosen? And you choose *her*?"

He drew his arm down and clasped my hand, twining his fingers tightly with mine. "We chose each other long ago."

An expression of surprising sadness swept Charlotte's features. "Then it's a fight to the death, because—"

"Because?" Ronan's voice was gentle. "Do you even remember why you're so angry? What more could you want? You have power. Strength. Immortality."

"I want to win."

"Then I can't help you," Ronan said sadly. "I can't watch this." He caught my eye. His voice had gone hoarse. "Just...be merciful."

He squeezed my hand once more, and I couldn't peel my eyes from him as he left the room.

I'd make this okay for him. I had to.

It was just me and Charlotte. And the misericordia. The metal seemed to pulse in my hand.

"You heard him. Make it fast, little girl." She flicked her eyes to my blade. "It's obviously not a fair fight."

But I didn't budge. Instead, I let the silence hang. This was someone whom Ronan once loved more than anyone. How does somebody change so much? How did it go so wrong? Why had Charlotte become...*this*?

I sighed. "Tell me one thing. Why do you need to win so badly? It seems like you expend so much energy trying to be the favorite of one vampire or another. Dagursson, Fournier, Jacob...who's next? Why not just please yourself? Who cares if you don't win everything? Winning might not matter so much if you changed the game."

"Says the girl who's a loser."

I shrugged. "If leaving here with my life and people I love makes me a loser, then great. So be it. I haven't lost if I have someone like Ronan by my side."

Her eyes glittered with anger...but did I see jealousy there, too? "You get my brother," she said acidly. "You've made that abundantly clear."

"I think you've been away from humanity for too long, Charlotte. Ronan isn't a zero-sum game. He can love his family and me at the same time. In fact, he wants nothing more than to have you in his life. From the very beginning, he talked so much about you that I was even a little jealous, which has got to be the stupidest thing ever, seeing as you're his sister and he thought you were dead at the time."

Her expression cracked as she let out a quick gasp of a laugh. But then her face hardened back to its perfect shell once more. "I'm not good at sharing."

My voice softened. For an instant, I'd seen Charlotte in there, Ronan's Charlotte, the vulnerable, lonely girl. "Sharing's pretty nice, actually. Without it, you're alone. Is that what you really want?"

Anguish was quicksilver in her eyes, and then it flashed to rage. "What I want is for you to finish this." She strode forward, getting in my face. Snatching my hand in hers, she pulled the point of my blade against the soft flesh beneath her own chin.

I tried to tug my hand back, but she drew it closer to her throat, pressing it to her skin until it began to sizzle. Her face crumpled in pain. And something told me it wasn't her imminent death that was the unbearable thing. "Just...do it. Fast and easy." She peeled her lips into a snarl. "Before I turn this blade on you."

Amid her rage, I saw flickers of the deepest sorrow. She'd been as broken by these vampires as I had. Ronan was right—the little girl who'd chased crabs at the seashore was in there somewhere. And she loved him still.

I stepped even closer to her. It gave me a better angle with my blade arm. "Nothing's easy. I've learned that the hard way." I twisted, and my wrist broke free of her grip, though I kept the misericordia in place. "Now shut up and listen." I pushed slightly, and her flesh smoked. "You won't look for us. You'll stay in your dark little world. And if you ever cross my path in anger again, Charlotte, I swear, my face will be the last thing you ever see."

I swung my arm around and slammed the base of the misericordia on the side of her head, right on her temple. She toppled to the ground like dead weight, and I nudged her with my toe to make certain she was unconscious. "Don't ever say I wasn't fair."

The sight of Ronan slumped and leaning sideways in the hallway, facing away from the door—it broke my heart.

I went to him. Hesitated for a moment, then put a hand on the small of his back.

It was such a pleasure to be able to touch him like this. That it was my prerogative now to take such liberties.

He turned, and I was met by those haunted eyes I loved so much. "Is it done?"

"I love you too much to kill your sister." I took his hand, and the amazed, relieved expression that collapsed his features brought tears to my eyes. I laughed through them. "But I swear, if she comes for me, I'll cut a bitch."

A startled laugh escaped him. "Language, Ms. Drew." Then he leaned down and kissed me.

By the time he pulled back, I was beaming. "I could get used to this."

He put a single finger beneath my chin. "You'd best. And now, as someone I'm quite fond of might say, let's finish this thing."

CHAPTER TWENTY-FIVE

Ronan cracked the door and whispered, "Follow me."

I grabbed a handful of his shirt to hold him back. "Can you make it? You could barely stand a minute ago."

He nodded. "I don't know what she got me with, but it's metabolizing fast." He tipped my face up to look at him. "Ann, we have no choice. We have to move now. The Synod is holding your mother several floors down. If we have any hope of saving her and getting out of here alive, we need to move before they can rally more guards."

"This place goes even deeper under the water?" I shuddered.

He pulled me along the hallway. "And here I thought you'd become quite the sea nymph."

I caught up to jog by his side. "It's a wonder I'm not more traumatized, seeing as someone threw me in deep water before I was ready."

"I wanted to see you in a wetsuit," he said with a wicked grin.

I tripped over my feet, then scampered to catch back up to

him, my cheeks burning. I remembered that day very well. Him, unzipping my suit. Me, mortified in my two piece. His fingers grazing my skin. He'd planned it that way?

All I managed to say was, "Oh."

He shot me a quick, knowing smile.

Who knew Ronan had game?

We turned off into a small back corridor, and he led me through a thick metal door into an industrial-looking stairwell.

"Service stairs," he whispered.

"So there are back stairs." It made me think of my friends. Where were they now? Had they gotten free? I hoped they were all okay.

He held up a hand to pause the conversation and tilted his head, listening. "Sounds clear. Down we go."

I'd expected a Medieval dungeon, but this floor had the same industrial feel as the main factory. With white-painted cinderblock walls, plain gray flooring, and fluorescent lights humming overhead, we could be in any hospital basement anywhere.

"It has all the charm of a morgue," I said. "Or prison, maybe?"

"Because it is both those things." Ronan grabbed me abruptly and pulled me into an alcove, his hand over my mouth.

Footsteps.

He held me tightly as someone walked past, the *click-click* of their shoes echoing along the cold, empty hall.

And it felt so good to have him clutching me like that, I forgot to be nervous.

He let go, and it took me a second to catch my breath. He must've spied some look on my face, because he leaned down and landed a quick kiss on my cheek. "You make this difficult.

But I need you to concentrate. Then we will have all the time in the world for me to put that look on your face."

I felt a blush flame from my forehead to my toes. But I nodded. He was right.

Concentrate.

"There's a small infirmary through the double doors at the end of this corridor," he continued. "They're holding your mother there."

"In an infirmary?"

"They're keeping her alive, but don't misunderstand. Their intention isn't for her to get better. She's a permanent feeder. The good news is, she's too valuable for them to let her die. She's weak, but she'll be in decent trim."

"That's…" Tears sprang to my eyes. That existence was no existence at all. Thinking of my mother in there, thinking that was what the Synod had wanted for *me*…it was unimaginable. Horrifying. "We have to help her."

"We will," he said fiercely. "We are. We must be quick, though. There aren't many places to hide on this level. When we step out, we sprint to the end of the hall. Quietly and quickly, aye? Quiet and quick gets us out alive."

"Got it," I told him, my voice tight. And it was true, as long as I had him, I had this.

He poked his head out to make sure it was clear, then we were out like a shot. Through the double doors.

We found ourselves in what looked like a small hospital ward. There were several closed doors and not a guard in sight. I tugged Ronan's arm, and he leaned down for me to whisper in his ear. "Where is everyone?"

He whispered in mine, "You must've caused quite the stir." But I'd melted a little at the feel of his warm breath on my skin, and he pulled back to demand, "This is you concentrating?"

"Sorry, sorry. Go on."

"If the others have discovered Jacob and the Synod are dead, they'd have called all the guards to the upper floors."

"You picked some badass Acari for your team."

"The best," he said proudly.

He cared for those girls, I realized. It was clear. It'd been clear in the way he'd helped me when I'd first arrived. How he'd helped others, as he could.

We began peeking in rooms, and the sight that met me behind each closed door chilled me. There were women of all ages, incapacitated. Hooked to IVs. Barely conscious. "Can't we do something?"

"We can't save them all, Ann."

We tiptoed past what looked like an abandoned nurse's station, and I froze.

"What are you doing?" he mouthed.

My legs folded under me. I'd heard a voice I recognized. A voice I knew so very well.

Carden was here. He was talking to someone.

Ronan knelt and grabbed me, tucking us both under a desk.

I wanted to get to my mother, but I also wanted to eavesdrop, to hear what he was doing here. See if I could glimpse the true Carden.

There was a woman's voice.

"Freya," Ronan mouthed.

I leaned to whisper in his ear. "What are they doing here?"

He shrugged, before putting his mouth to my own ear. "Maybe he's trying to save your mother? Save you? Who knows with McCloud?"

"There were all kinds of ways he could've saved me about thirty minutes ago," I grumbled. "I'd have appreciated that more."

He pulled back and put a calming hand on my forearm. "Just listen," he mouthed, but I'd seen triumph flicker in his eyes. Carden wasn't with me, but *he* was, and apparently, it was where he'd wanted to be all along.

Freya's voice rose in anger, carrying clearly down the empty hall. "I will continue to rule *Eilean Ban-Laoch* and you will take the Isle."

"What of Alcántara?" Carden asked.

"The Spaniard is like a dog with a bone, clinging to the past. He is stubborn, self-important, and ill-behaved. He tries to play both sides, as when he refused to relinquish Annelise. I say let him be with his books. He'll be only too happy to let you take control publicly so that he might remain sequestered among his papers, thinking he is controlling things from the shadows."

"*Me* control the Isle?"

"Yes, *you*, Carden. You could be the face of *Eyja næturinnar*. Yours is a strong face, a new face."

I heard it in his voice—Carden wanted to rule. What had he thought this would mean for me?

As for Alcántara...that was a surprise. Was he truly more interested in books than anything else? Ironically, it probably meant that, all this time, he'd been interested in me for my mind after all.

It didn't matter to me either way. I had zero desire to see the Spanish vampire ever again.

As for Carden, I had to look at his face one last time. I wanted to know what I might see there.

I crawled from our hiding spot. Stood up.

And Ronan was right beside me. He'd clearly read my mind, because he grumbled, "Must we?"

"We must." I followed the sound of Carden's voice. It led to a nursing office, where he stood speaking with Freya and Lilac. I took in the scene, feeling confused. Had he always been this close with Freya? With *Lilac*? I raised my voice to carry, saying, "This seems cozy."

I'd taken them by surprise, and it gave me a perverse pleasure.

"There you are, my dove." Carden looked genuinely happy to see me.

It made me feel a bit more at ease, and I realized how nervous I'd been to face him. As if Carden might not be on my side after all. But still, as Carden took a step toward me, I took a step back.

"What are you doing in here?" I asked warily.

"I came to bargain for your mother."

Lilac sat on the edge of a desk, swinging her legs. "We were invited to partake in the special refreshments. Jacob was *so* flattered by our offering."

Carden shot a look at Freya. "Keep that girl quiet."

Ronan eyed them one by one, then said to Carden, "It's reassuring to see how you were doing all you could to save Annelise."

"This *is* saving Annelise, pup."

Ronan nodded, but he didn't look convinced. "Mmhmm."

Carden looked from Ronan to me and back again. "The real question is, what is going on *here*?"

"We're going to save her mother. And then we're just going."

Carden's focus turned to me. "You're going?" I didn't know what he saw, but his eyes went flat. "I see." He tipped his head. "You say you will go. And yet, you know I cannot."

Freya tsked at me. "Silly girl. Surely you understand the implications of what has been set in motion here. For the first time in centuries, the end of infighting is in sight. Balance is almost restored. You'd be a fool to leave him. To leave your sister," she said with a glance to Lilac. "You could claim your place on either island. If it weren't for Carden, who seems to believe he's your protector, I'd *make* you claim your place."

"My place is far from your islands," I told her. I wasn't even in the mood to address the whole Lilac thing. As it was, I was bummed to have to leave here with her still standing.

My gaze returned to Carden. I was nursing some hurt feelings, which was absurd. Protector or not, I was leaving him. I'd chosen Ronan. Why should I care if he wanted to make his permanent home on the Isle of Night? But I couldn't resist saying, "I didn't realize you liked the Isle so much."

"It is my destiny to rule *Eyja næturinnar*," he said in complete earnest.

"Have fun with that."

Carden's voice grew firm. "There are those on the Isle who are good."

"Yeah? Name three."

"I will find more good there, Annelise. I've been given much in this world. I must give back. It's who I am." He gestured to the ward outside the door. "I must fight against atrocities like this."

My heart lightened a shade. "You'll save these women?"

He tipped his head gravely. "As I can."

Such a Carden response.

I went from feeling melancholy to simple exhaustion. "Well, try."

"Stay with me," Carden rasped, his tone gone urgent. "I'll make you my queen."

"I've never been one for titles," I said, stupidly trying to joke it off, but completely nonsensically, I began to choke up. "I...I'm with Ronan. I think I've always had feelings for him." Carden's face began to shutter and I pitched my voice with every bit of earnestness that I could. "I'm sorry. I think you and I both knew. But it doesn't mean I didn't care for you. You meant so much to me—you still do. You got me through. For a while, you were my everything."

"But no longer?"

"It's not who I am, Carden. That's not the person I want to be."

He put a finger on my lips. "Enough. I understand. As you must understand, this is my life. I am Vampire. And you, my dearest, are not."

He was being gracious and kind, and it reminded me why I'd adored him so. "I wish you all the best, Carden. Do some good on the Isle. No more Directorate Challenges, okay? But you belong with your kind. And so does this." I leaned down and pulled the misericordia from my boot, placing it in his hands. At the sound of Freya's gasp, I wrapped his fingers tightly around the hilt. "You're the only vampire I'd ever trust with this thing. But I want you to have it."

His eyes widened, full of emotion, then met mine. "Always you surprise, love." He carefully touched the misericordia to his heart then his forehead with a bow. "And always I will be here for you."

Freya smirked. "Always is a long time for a vampire."

But Carden didn't take the bait. "We Scots have steadfast hearts," he told me solemnly. "You must go now. It won't be long before the guards return. The time has come for my dove to fly." He pulled me into a hug. In it, was warmth and affection...and goodbye. "Go get your Birgit.".

"That is not what we discussed," Freya snapped.

Carden seemed to expand before my eyes. "There will be no discussion," he snarled. "As *Eyja næturinnar*'s new leader, I decree it. None will be kept against their will any longer."

Freya bristled at his adamance. "I hope you know what you're doing."

Carden ignored her and took my hand, giving it one last squeeze. "Last door on the left. We'll guard the corridor."

"We will?" I heard Lilac complain, but Ronan and I were already on our way.

"You okay?" Ronan asked as we stood outside my mother's room.

I nodded. "I kind of am, actually."

He tipped his head toward her door. "Nervous?"

"Yeah." I gave a tight laugh. "Weirdly so. What if she doesn't like me?"

He took my shoulders and turned me to face him. "You've faced horrors of the sort most people can't conceive. You've fought enemies of every stripe—Acari, Trainee, Draug, Vampire—and triumphed. You've helped change the face of the Isle." He placed his palm on the hospital room door. "But this? This is a woman who left you only against her will. A woman who loves you."

"I don't have a lot of experience with that," I said, voice cracking.

"You're a quick study," Ronan said gently. His eyes were soft and loving on me. "Don't be afraid, Ann. I'm right here."

"I know." I reached for his hand. "I get that now."

His other hand went to the door. "It's time to meet your mother."

EPILOGUE

During his years of travel as a Tracer, Ronan built up an extensive list of contacts. Powerful ones, who know the value of powerful friends. With their help, we made our way to an island. A very different kind of island.

A tropical one.

Ronan assures me we'll be safe here. Vampires despise sunlight, and there's plenty of sunlight in the French Caribbean. There's sun shining down, rays of light glittering along the water, and a beautiful, white glare beating up at us from the sandy soil. No sensible vampire would dare step foot on any of these islands.

Even if one did, they'd have a hard time tracking us down. Ronan tells me that, through the years, several Acari and Tracers have made safe escapes to this very part of the world.

Including the feeders on Melkøya. Carden, in Carden fashion, was as good as his word, and he freed every last woman. He found and helped my friends, too, and all but Guidon Mala made it alive off that grim rock. The rest were offered their freedom, and most took it. Except for Monique and Clara, who returned to the Isle of Night. There's no figuring some people, I guess. But the rest—Juliet, Regina, and Kenzie—they're out there somewhere. Maybe not even far from us.

Not that we'd ever be able to find them.

But I'm not feeling short on friends or life. It's warm and easygoing here, and Ronan and I spend time beach combing or cooking or wandering the Saturday market. We read a lot, and yes, we do the crossword every day.

He's squirreled away money through the years. Not so much that we can live large, but it's enough that we never return from the market without him buying me some trinket—a blue beaded necklace, red scarf, golden bangles—with no gray, black, or navy in sight. Our latest find was a purple and orange sarong with small, shining metal disks sewn on the ends. I wear it tied it around my waist, where it shimmers and flows against my tanned legs.

My mother is with us, but she spends her days on the water. She likes to set sail, often for weeks at a time. But she always comes back to us. She says she will always come back.

She laughs the most wonderful belly laughs when I tell her my stories of water, about my old phobias—it all seems so distant now. Her laugh makes me laugh, too. It makes it all okay.

There's a university on the other side of the island, and I've been thinking of starting classes this fall. No more Germanic languages for me, though. And math has definitely lost its charms. I was thinking something scientific. I watch research boats take off from the docks, and think maybe it's just cold water that scares me. I want to be productive, somewhere sunny and open, near to those creatures who swim free.

Ronan assures me matriculation won't be a problem this time, though I jokingly tell him he's not allowed within twenty feet of their registrar's office. I am losing the surname Drew, though. That was the name of the man whose Florida apartment I lived in—an abusive man, not my father.

Ronan wants me to take his name. Munro. It means mountain, which strikes me as fitting. It's a good name, an old name. But I'm making him wait for my answer.

As for Carden, I was sad to say goodbye. But he has his cause and his goals, and they have nothing to do with me and everything to do with a world I was desperate to leave far behind.

A world I *have* left far behind.

I have a new world, and it's headed my way right now.

Ronan.

He raises his knees high, stepping out of the surf, his board in hand. And let me say: I do not miss that wetsuit one bit. Water glistens over his body and weighs down his low-slung board shorts. He's brown from the sun, with a bit of extra red just along the bridge of his nose. He whips the wet hair from his forehead and gives me a questioning grin. "What are you cooking in that brilliant mind of yours?"

It takes me a second to answer. What *was* I thinking? That I never knew I could be so happy?

Finally, I tell him, "I'm thinking your tattoo is all wrong."

He gives me a quick, baffled look, then studies his arm and the Proust quote he'd inked along his bicep. *Le seul paradis c'est le paradis perdu.*

The flex and shift of his body never ceases to mesmerize me. He catches my eye and the naughty glint in his tells me he's read my mind. "What is it, Ann?" he asks innocently. "Lost your taste for French novels, or is it me that's troubling you?"

I give him my best saucy smile. "You may be trouble, Ronan, but you never trouble me." Then I reread the words on his arm, wanting to get my thoughts just right. *The only paradise is paradise lost.*

"No," I say as I gaze up at him. "It's that...my only paradise is right here."

His cheek twitches with some strong emotion, and my heart swells to see such affection, such affinity.

I'm his. He's mine. It makes us vulnerable, but we're safe with each other in our new world.

He lays his surfboard in the sand and reaches a hand down to me. "Come, love," he whispers.

I take his hand and lean into him, digging my feet into the warm, powdery sand. We begin a leisurely walk.

Into our new life.

———

Read on for an excerpt from the first book in The Pressing Dark Duology by Veronica Wolff.

PREVIEW OF ACROSS THE PRESSING DARK

Lost in time, bound by love, hunted by magic.

At nineteen, Rose thought tracking down her unpredictable mother in Scotland would be her biggest challenge. Instead, she's ripped from her time and thrust into the unforgiving Highlands of the seventeenth century, where she becomes entangled in deadly clan rivalries, ancient magic, and a history she was never meant to uncover.

Irresistibly drawn to Callum, a young Scotsman trapped by fate and servitude, Rose finds a connection unlike any she has ever known. But their growing love puts them both in mortal peril. Dark forces gather, wielding powerful sorcery to keep them apart, and Rose must decide: return to her own time, or risk everything to forge a future with Callum?

A sweeping tale of love, sacrifice, and magic, *Across the Pressing Dark* is the first book in a romantic young adult time-travel duology—where love defies time, and the past is never truly buried.

> "Wolff transports the reader into
> a wondrous world of chivalry and adventure."
> – *Fresh Fiction on LORD OF THE HIGHLANDS*

> "Veronica Wolff's Scotsmen are pure temptation!"
> – *New York Times bestselling author Sandra Hill on*
> *LORD OF THE HIGHLANDS*

> "Veronica Wolff is a fresh, exciting voice in Scottish
> time-travel–a supernova in the making."
> – *Penelope Williamson on WARRIOR OF THE HIGHLANDS*

> "Wolff writes a story that will grab you
> from the first word and not let go."
> – *Night Owl Reviews on DEVIL'S HIGHLANDER,*
> *Reviewer Top Pick*

My bag hits the floor with a hollow smack that ricochets off the dank stone walls of the inn. "Gone? What do you mean, gone?"

Where on earth is my mother?

The young receptionist doesn't look up. She just nods at the bill, filing her nails with a bored shrug. "We take cash or card, miss."

My mother ditched me. I don't know why I'm surprised. It's kind of her thing. Edinburgh was just her latest disappearing act, and here I am, searching for her all over again. Only this time, I'm in a foreign country.

"We'll go to Scotland," she told me out of the blue. "Tour that school you like." We saved up for months, or at least *I* did. Heaven forbid Janet work a day in her life. But still, this was supposed to be *our* trip together. Our first *anything* together. A mother-daughter bonding moment. Just a quick jaunt during midterm break, a long weekend in late October.

I should be home by now, studying for exams. Instead, I'm chasing after *her*.

My eyes blur, anger threatening to slide into the familiar dejection that defined my childhood. I pinch the bridge of my nose, hard. I will not cry in front of this stranger. Instead, I focus on the peeling sign over her head like I might be quizzed on it. THE MERRY WIDOW INN, ESTABLISHED 1605. Which, judging by the state of this place, is probably the last time anyone dusted.

Why did my mother come *here*? She hasn't been back to Scotland since before I was born. She refuses to talk about it.

Is *this* where she's from?

Not that I've had a chance to ask. Our first morning together, she went to the bathroom and never came back. I'd have called her cell phone, if she had one. She claims she doesn't believe in them, which is like not believing in the wheel, but whatever.

That was two days ago. I've been searching for her ever since…until this place called. "Janet Campbell is racking up a bill she can't pay." Four hours, one train, and two buses later, here I am. In the wilds of Scotland.

I missed my college tour, of course.

Just the thought of it makes my head ache. What else did I miss? Was I supposed to have an interview?

I didn't even get to see the campus. The physics department at the University of Edinburgh is world famous. It's my dream to transfer there. But instead of exploring the school, I spent two days scouring every pub while staving off panic attacks. More than ever, I need to get away from my mother. Study abroad. Worry about nothing and nobody but myself for once.

But first, I have to find her.

I glance at the invoice. Nausea rolls through me. "Um, okay. This is...okay." I chew my thumbnail, trying to figure out what to do. "But you said you know where Janet is? *Janet Campbell.*" I say her name extra slowly, like the problem here is my accent and not basic human decency. "My name's Rose. You called me? You said she was here."

The receptionist finally looks up. Expression flat. Unimpressed. "She's nae here. Not anymore. Just the bill." She slides the paper forward, tapping the total with a bright red nail. "Cash or card."

This was supposed to be *my* moment.

All my old classmates have moved on, but I stayed home to help my grandfather with the farm. Poppa says we can afford for me to go away to school, but there's always something. Some crisis that drains our savings. And I've always—always—put everything aside to help.

But this?

This is next-level Janet. Worse than the time I missed my calc exam to drive three hours and bail her out of jail. (Indecent exposure. A music festival. Don't ask.) I'm almost twenty. An adult. I need my own life. I don't even know what that looks like. But I do know it's not minding my mother or tending Poppa's animals.

So I've done everything I can. Worked my butt off. Taken every possible science and math class at the community college. And this trip? It'd finally felt like Janet was doing something for *me*. Supporting me.

How wrong I was. It was never about me. It was just another way for her to get what she wants.

She always gets what she wants.

"Um, okay." I try to buy time, because I have no idea what to do next. "We were supposed to go home yesterday. I already had to change our flights once. It's not cheap."

No reaction.

"We came all the way from New York."

Silence.

"Like...in America?"

The receptionist's nail file stops mid-stroke. She gives me a slack-jawed scowl. "I ken where New York is."

I rub my arms. I'm tired and cold, and I swear, it feels like it's actually wet in here. "Well, Janet's my mother, and—"

A laugh explodes from her. "Your *mum*?" Her eyes shine as she scans me, head to toe, like she's just realizing something. "Well, your mum fair showed our lads a good time. Singing and carrying on in the pub. One too many pints, I hear."

Heat flares in my cheeks. "Yeah, sorry," I mumble. If *carrying on* were an Olympic sport, Janet would be a gold medalist.

"The woman wouldnae even tell us where she lives." The receptionist leans against the desk, smirking. "We had to look through her things to find your number. That's how we got you."

My stomach tightens.

"I thought old Dan—this is his place, aye?—I thought he might have a cardiac when he learned the woman's from America. Your mum's accent is as Scottish as a square sausage. The man was besotted. I was beginning to think he might propose." She stops filing, pins me with a sudden, assessing stare. Then she shakes her head and lets out another explosive laugh. "And she's your *mum*."

Like it's the funniest thing she's ever heard.

"Yep." I force a smile through gritted teeth. "My mom."

Dan wouldn't be Janet's first proposal. She stands out. Always has. She's movie-star beautiful—fresh-faced, delicate, luminous. Like a porcelain doll.

But, wow, is she ugly on the inside.

My whole life, she's been consumed by one thing: herself. Her desires. Her beauty. She's the only star in her personal sky, and that star is a black hole, insatiable for an ever-growing list of esoteric demands. Poppa once said she's selfish as a fox and twice as sly.

Poor Poppa. My grandfather didn't know what hit him when Janet showed up on his doorstep, newly married to his son. She and my father met during a whirlwind weekend at some Scottish music festival. They were only supposed to stay at Poppa's farm while they got on their feet, but then my father died when I was a baby.

And Janet—with no family, no job, no plan—never left. Poppa took her in. Took *us* in. It's been just the three of us ever since. I wouldn't have survived my mother without him.

I mean, it wasn't all bad. There were times when my mother was pure magic. She was the mom who'd call in sick for me with elaborate stories about exotic diseases so we could spend the day at the zoo instead. She was particularly delighted by the chimps who'd throw their poop at the tourists. Those days, she made me feel important, like her co-conspirator.

By middle school, I knew she wasn't like other moms. But it was my eleventh birthday when she stopped being *Mom* and became *Janet*. She promised a massive party— balloons, a sundae bar, pony rides. She invited my whole class.

And then...nothing.

No party. No presents. Just me, standing in our empty yard, apologizing to twenty confused kids.

But I still have to track her down. I mean, she *is* my mother. I need to find her before she gets into real trouble. Or bankrupts Poppa.

"So," I say, scanning the receptionist's name tag, "Annie. What do you think I should do? I have to find her." On a hunch, I add, "We're running out of money."

That sure gets her attention.

She starts ranting at me—something about a damaged room, an unpaid bar tab—but I've stopped listening. A strange click, followed by an eerie moan, echoes around me. There's a moment's whirring. Then—bells.

My breath catches. I turn. A hulking grandfather clock looms in the corner, carved from wood so dark it's nearly black.

Bong. The sound is slow, deep, rolling through the inn like the groan of some slumbering beast.

I gaze at the clock's ancient face. It's mottled yellow-brown, the Roman numerals faded but legible. A small dial in the center tracks the sun and moon. Four o'clock. Not quite day. Not quite night. The sun, poised to sink, grins at me. A broad, toothy leer, like a cartoon villain about to twirl his mustache.

Bong. The second toll thrums in my ribs. Something about this moment feels wrong. Familiar, but wrong.

Bong. A strange, bewildering grief wells up, sudden and unshakable.

Bong. The last chime stretches long, lazily fading into silence. The hour hand clicks into place with a decisive *snick.*

Annie's voice yanks me back. "Hae you got it?"

I blink hard, shaking my head as I force myself to look away from the clock. "Sorry, yeah. I'll pay for her room. Or whatever."

I just need to hold it together a little longer. I've been running on anxiety, adrenaline, and Diet Coke, and I'm beyond exhausted. I shake out my ice-cold hands, then scoop up my bag. "I'd like one, too. A room, I mean. Please."

Annie narrows her eyes. Mascara clumps her lashes into thick, blue-black spikes. "You'll need to pay for both."

"Yeah, of course."

I swing my backpack around, dig for my wallet, and hand her my debit card. I'm genuinely astounded when it works.

Thank you, Poppa.

He must've put money in my account. Even though we don't have a penny to spare, he always looks out for me.

I take my key and head down a dark-paneled hallway, the air instantly growing cooler. Shadows press close as I climb the narrow staircase. Every step groans, ancient floorboards creaking beneath my weight. By the time I enter my room, dread sits heavy on my shoulders.

I lock my door. Jiggle the handle. Check it again.

Just in case.

The decor doesn't exactly put me at ease. It's like a Scottish tourist shop exploded, vomiting plaid everywhere. Red plaid carpet, blue plaid blankets, yellow-and-brown plaid curtains. The room is small, musty. But I guess it's clean enough. And yet...there's a sensation I can't quite place.

Like something is watching me.

Listening.

I shake it off. I'm being ridiculous.

It's my mother's fault. Or rather, the song she used to sing me. I haven't thought about it in years, but ever since I saw signs for Loch Lomond, it's been looping in my head. "O ye'll take the high road, and I'll take the low road, and I'll be in Scotland afore ye, but me and my true love will never meet again, on the bonnie, bonnie banks of Loch Lomond..."

The tiny me had adored it. A story of true love, like a prince and princess in a fairy tale. Until the day Janet announced its true meaning.

She was good at that. Ruining things.

"It was sung by a prisoner," she said. Even now, I remember her voice—low, strangely gleeful. The way it scared me.

"Captured by his enemies, he was. The lad knew he was to die in the morning. So he sang a song to his love." Janet leaned in close, watching me. "He'd take the low road. And only then could he meet her again."

I didn't understand at first.

"The low road," she whispered. "The one the ghosties travel." She waited, watched my face, let it sink in. Then burst into peals of laughter when it did.

I never let her sing it again after that.

And now it's back in my head, spooking me. "Relax," I say, extra loud, and shattering the silence makes me feel better.

I'm just overtired. It's making me dramatic.

I toss my phone onto the side table and drop onto the bed. The mattress is thin and feels almost slightly damp, but I'm too beat to care. Maybe I'll just close my eyes for a few minutes before figuring out dinner. I don't even bother changing. I just kick off my shoes, crawl under the yellowed sheets, pull the scratchy wool blanket to my chin, and pass out.

My eyes flick open into darkness.

Something has woken me.

I fumble for my phone on the nightstand. It lights up at my touch. 2:19 a.m.

There's a voicemail from Poppa. I tap it.

And the battery dies. Because of course.

With a groan, I stretch over the edge of the bed, flailing my arm blindly until my fingers graze my backpack. I drag it closer. Dig around. And it hits me: I must've left my power adapter at the hostel in Edinburgh. I raced out of there so fast when I got the call about Janet.

I grab the cord instead and wriggle it into the USB outlet on the lamp, and why does that never work until the third try? I finally get it, and...nothing. I wait a minute, but the little charging symbol never appears. No surprise, this ancient building probably has sketchy wiring to go with its creaky stairs.

I flop back onto the mattress and try to make my body relax, but it's no good. I'm wide awake.

With a sigh, I swing my feet onto the floor. I didn't shut the curtains before passing out, and the glassy black rectangle of window draws me toward it.

Pressing my forehead to the cool glass, I peer outside. The night is still. Heavy. It wraps around the inn, thick and silent. Somehow, it comforts me. Reminds me of home.

This land, as lush and remote as Poppa's farm, fills me with a deep, familiar peace. The similarities steady me. Make me feel less alone.

Outside, the moon hangs pale in the darkness.

A new moon.

I learned about them in astronomy class. It's when you see the side of the moon that's not lit by the sun. Faint and gray, it hovers in the sky like the ghost of itself.

A knot in my chest begins to loosen. I take a deep breath. Exhale slowly. It feels so good, I do it again. Deeper. Slower.

Cheek pressing against the glass, I crane my neck, searching till I find Loch Lomond. It gleams in the distance like a bead of mercury. I pull back, soothed.

And then—a man. In the window.

I shriek, stumble back. He's young, maybe a few years older

than me, his silhouette stark against the night sky. But I'm on the second floor.

He can't be outside. Which means it's his reflection. *He's behind me.*

Pulse slamming, I spin and stumble back, knocking my head on the glass as my eyes dart around the room. It's empty. Holding my breath, I brace a hand on the sill and force myself to look back at the window.

He's still there.

Impossible.

Outside, there's nothing but a two-story drop.

Which means...*a ghost?* No. That's ridiculous. Right? But he *feels* like a ghost. And he's looking at me. Watching me.

An unexpected sense of peace washes over me. I should be terrified. Screaming, running, calling for help.

But I'm not.

There's something about his presence that feels familiar somehow. Safe. The only thing that scares me is that he might look away. Somehow, in his gaze, I feel known. Seen. Down to my soul.

I don't want him to disappear.

We study each other. Who was he? *When* was he?

His shirt is old-fashioned—laced at the neck and smudged with dirt, like he wiped his hand down the front. Dark hair falls messily to his collar. Even in the foggy reflection, I can tell he's strong. Tough. Like he's got bigger things to worry about than clothing and hair.

"Who are you?" My voice is barely a whisper.

And yet, his eyes snap to mine, corners narrowing with intensity. His gaze is a force, a weight, like it might bore through time to reach me. Charisma rolls off him, an invisible thread pulled tight between us.

He mouths something, but all I hear is silence.

"What?"

He tries again, frustration creasing his brow. Shaking his head, his lips form words he needs me to understand.

A surge of heat prickles my chest as his anguish pierces me, sharp and insistent. His need becomes my own. I press my palms to the cold glass, like I could reach through time itself to touch him.

It's too much. I squeeze my eyes shut.

When I open them again, he's gone.

Buy ACROSS THE PRESSING DARK

ACKNOWLEDGMENTS

With special thanks to the following people:

Martha White, treasured friend, secret weapon, and the person most likely to be called in the event of my incarceration. And to the rest of our beloved YA posse: Ingrid Paulson, Whitney Miller, and Heidi Kling.

Professional me wants to thank Jeannie Ruesch, creator of gorgeous covers, at The Theater of Marketing. Danielle Poiesz and her copyediting talents at Double Vision Editorial. And the fabulous Lisa Rogers, who seems blessedly undaunted by my panicked emails.

Thanks to my primary cheering section, alpha readers, and chief brainstormers, Mom, Clara, Owen, Joey, Sue, and Adam. Especially Adam. Always, Adam.

And finally, dear readers, I want to thank YOU. I don't know if I can fully express how much your messages mean to me. Your online notes (and nudges!) never fail to make my day. This book is truly for you. <3.

Highland Heroes

Time Travel Romance

Master of the Highlands

Sword of the Highlands

Warrior of the Highlands

Lord of the Highlands

The Pressing Dark

Young Adult Time Travel Romance

Across the Pressing Dark

Beyond the Bounds

Ballad of a Bonnie Rogue

Novellas

The Drowning Sea

ABOUT THE AUTHOR

Veronica Wolff is an award-winning, bestselling author who likes monsters, fight scenes, and first kisses. Sometimes all at the same time. She lived everywhere from Texas, to Hawaii, to India, before finally settling in Northern California, where she lives with her husband, two kids, and a small menagerie of rescued pets. She writes in several genres, including Scottish historical romance, time travel, contemporary romance, and young adult.

Veronica Wolff
Where you'll find me:
https://veronicawolff.com
https://veronicawolff.com/newsletter/
https://www.goodreads.com/author/show/1140298.
Veronica_Wolff

instagram.com/veronicawolff

facebook.com/VeronicaWolffFanPage

bookbub.com/authors/veronica-wolff

amazon.com/Veronica-Wolff/e/B001ILMBMK

bsky.app/profile/veronicawolff.bsky.social

www.ingramcontent.com/pod-product-compliance
Lightning Source LLC
Chambersburg PA
CBHW050612190726
48283CB00007B/2392

Lenox Winter is the son of rock royalty. Although born into the London elite, his laid-back style and relaxed vibe has always made him feel better suited for something or somewhere outside of the legacy his parents have built. Some place where the sun shines all year long and the people move to a different beat. Ibiza.

Far away from the busy streets and dreary skies of London rests the white isle. Home to hedonism, immaculate sandy beaches, and utter tranquility. While holidaying on the island with a group of his best friends, and desperate to leave behind the stresses of London as well as the harmful memories of his ex, he meets Lyric; a man who epitomises the bohemian vibe of his beloved Ibiza.

As romance quickly blossoms between the two, Lenox begins to feel that he may have finally found someone special to help him escape the suffocating clutches of his life in the UK. But when things take a drastic turn, both begin to realise that there are two sides to every person and that some things are better kept hidden.

Sunburnt is a story of romance, intrigue, and deep twisted secrets that takes the idea of a holiday romance to catastrophic new heights.

A NineStar Press Publication

Published by NineStar Press
P.O. Box 91792,
Albuquerque, New Mexico, 87199 USA.
www.ninestarpress.com

Sunburnt

ISBN: 978-1-947904-71-2

Printed in the USA
First Edition
December, 2017

Also available in eBook

ISBN: 978-1-947904-61-3

Warning: This book contains sexually explicit content, which may only be suitable for mature readers graphic violence, and the death of a MC. It also has no HEA..